WARNING:
O NOT GIVE THIS BOOK TO YOUR OWN GRANDMA. SHE MIGHT GET IDEAS.

ORCHARD BOOKS

First published in Great Britain in 2019 by The Watts Publishing Group

1 3 5 7 9 10 8 6 4 2

Text copyright © Kita Mitchell 2019
Illustrations © Nathan Reed 2019
The moral rights of the author and illustrator have been asserted.

A CIP catalogue record for this book
is available from the British Library.

ISBN 978 1 40835 552 7

Printed and bound in Great Britain by
Clays Ltd, St Ives plc / CPI Group (UK) Ltd, Croydon, CR0 4YY

The paper and board used in this book are
made from wood from responsible sources.

Orchard Books
An imprint of Hachette Children's Group
Part of The Watts Publishing Group Limited
Carmelite House
50 Victoria Embankment
London EC4Y 0DZ

An Hachette UK Company
www.hachette.co.uk
www.hachettechildrens.co.uk

GRANDMA DANGEROUS AND THE TOE OF TREACHERY

By Kita Mitchell

Illustrated by Nathan Reed

ORCHARD

For Sophia, James and Iris

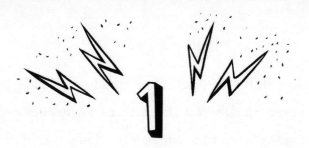

1

'**Let me get** this right,' I said. 'Dad's taking you on a surprise anniversary holiday and you're leaving me with <u>**GRANDMA BEATRIX?**</u>'

I waited for Mum to tell me she was joking, and that she wasn't really sending me to **Manners Manor** (as I like to call it) for a week.

But she didn't.

She just carried on packing her stuff.

'She's very excited.' Mum picked up a paperback and put it in her suitcase. 'She's got all sorts of things planned. You'll have a **lovely** time.'

'**No I won't**,' I said. 'I'll more likely **die of boredom**. Then you'll be sorry.'

'Don't be silly.' Mum peered into a

drawer. 'It'd take a lot longer than seven days to die of boredom. Do you think three swimsuits will be enough? I've no idea where your dad's taking me. No idea at all.' She picked up a travel brochure. 'Though I did find this on his desk. *Not that I was looking.*'

The brochure had a beach and a palm tree on the front, as well as two people with shiny white teeth, waving from the deck of a yacht.

It didn't look like the sort of thing Dad would book, to be honest – but I didn't bother saying, as I was still cross that I had to go to Grandma Beatrix's.

She's Mum's mum.

I call her **GRANDMA BORING**.

She's **awful**.

I don't think she means to be – but someone needs to tell her that **maths revision guides are not acceptable birthday gifts**.

She wears beige trouser suits, unless it's a special occasion, and then she wears a salmon one. Her blouses have bows at the neck, and her hair is very bouffant.

I've never seen it move. I don't know if it can.

She's overly fond of manners. Her finger starts wagging if I so much as think of putting an elbow on the table.

Or accidentally make a **slurping** noise.

Or drop a crumb.

Don't drop a crumb at Grandma Beatrix's house.

She can sense a stray crumb at a thousand paces. It's like her superpower.

If one falls off your plate, she'll fix it with her beady, crumb-spotting eyes, then zip round at the speed of light to brush it into her special, tabletop crumb dustpan.

'No harm done,' she'll say, as she tips it in the bin.

(If the crumb has jam on it, that's different. Jam involves a lot of tutting and a tablecloth change.)

It's not just manners. She's also fond of 'life skills'. Grandma Beatrix says they should be handed down from one generation to the next, and it's her absolute pleasure to pass them on.

It took several sessions, but I can now fold napkins into elegant swans. I also know there are many types of spoon, each with a different purpose. She promised that next time, we'd work on the forks. Forks, it seems, are complicated.

I closed my eyes. I didn't think I could bear it. 'Can't Grandma Florence look after me instead?' I asked. 'I wouldn't mind that.'

I wouldn't mind that at all. Grandma Florence is **SO** much fun. She's an explorer, like Dad. She's always up to something.

Mum calls her **<u>GRANDMA DANGEROUS</u>**.

She says she's a liability.

I admit it. Sometimes Grandma does lie, but she's not dangerous! She hasn't crashed her hot-air balloon for **ages**. The way Mum goes on, you'd think she did it all the time.

Mum's a health and safety officer. **She thinks walking down the street is risky**. She wants me to be an accountant, or a dentist. She definitely doesn't want me to be an explorer.

She's better than she used to be. Now I'm eleven, I'm allowed out by myself – but only because she put an app on my phone that shows her where I am. That's in case I get **KIDNAPPED**. I've never actually met a kidnapper, but Mum seems to think Great Potton is full of them, all lying in wait.

I've definitely inherited some explorer genes – but sometimes I wonder if they've been diluted by Mum's safety-conscious ones (for example, I don't like the dark and I'd generally prefer a sandwich to a grub). Grandma Florence says not to worry, and that explorer genes need to be developed. **Luckily, she's more than happy to help with that.**

Mum pushed in one last swimsuit and zipped up her case. 'I'm not asking Florence,' she said.

'Why not?'

'Ollie.' Mum gave me an exasperated look. 'It's Grandma Beatrix's turn. She's always complaining she doesn't see enough of you.'

Turn? I don't see why turns had anything to do with anything when a week of napkin folding was involved.

Mum went on. 'I'll enjoy the beach far more if I know you're safe, and not blowing something up.'

I scowled. Mum was always bringing up the firework in the trifle. **Just because a teeny bit of custard got on the ceiling**!

'I'm still finding glacé cherries in places they shouldn't be.'

I could see there was no point trying to change her mind.

I'd try Dad.

2

Dad was in his workshop. He was packing too.

He hadn't packed swimsuits and paperbacks though, like Mum.

No.

He'd packed **mosquito nets, night-vision goggles** and **a tranquilliser gun**.

I looked at the contents of his suitcase, and then I looked at him. 'Mum thinks you're taking her to a beach,' I said.

'**EXCELLENT**.' Dad looked delighted. 'I left a brochure out to throw her off the scent. She must have fallen for it.'

tranquilliser gun

night-vision goggles

mosquito net

'So you're **NOT**?'

'I am.' Dad busied himself with some emergency flares. '*Sort of.*'

'What do you mean, sort of?'

'We're flying **OVER** one,' Dad said.

I blinked. 'She's agreed to go in your plane?'

Dad snorted. '**Of course not**. Can you imagine?'

I don't know why Mum worries so much. Dad's plane is perfectly safe. He built it himself. It's amazing. It can fly halfway round the world on a single tank of peanut oil. He's only crashed it once – and that was into a swamp, which was nice and soft.

'We're getting a regular flight from Great Potton Airport,' Dad said.

'To where?' I asked. 'And why do you need that?' I pointed at the tranquilliser gun.

Dad perked up. 'Your mum's always saying I should be more safety-conscious. They were on offer at Explorer World. Two for one! If the tigers attack, we'll gain a few seconds.'

'**TIGERS?**' I blinked again.

'Yes. Your mum loves them.'

Mum did like tigers – but on tea towels, and mugs, mostly. I didn't say anything, though, as Dad was so excited.

'After the jungle we're potholing and cliff-jumping.' He slammed his case shut. 'I've bought her a **wingsuit**. She'll love it.'

I wasn't sure she would, to be honest.

I suddenly remembered why I'd come. 'Dad,' I said. 'Do I have to stay with Grandma Beatrix?'

He gave me a sympathetic pat. 'Sorry,' he said. 'It's her turn.'

●●●

It seemed I was going whether I liked it or not. I wasn't looking forward to it – but at least Grandma Beatrix had said I could take a friend.

I went to see if Piper wanted to come.

Piper's in my year at school. She's annoying, but we get on better than we used to. She's got loads of

13

brothers and sisters and today the twins were yelling their heads off, so we went into the garden.

'Are they supposed to sound like that?' I asked.

'They're teething.' Piper looked glum.

When I asked her if she wanted to come to Grandma's with me, she really liked the idea and said **'Yes, definitely,'** and whooped a lot.

I was quite surprised by that.

Then I realised she'd thought I meant Grandma Florence.

When I told her it was Grandma Beatrix, she wasn't so enthusiastic.

'You said your Grandma Beatrix was **awful**.' She glared at me. 'She checks you for nits.'

'I've **NEVER** said that,' I lied.

'I think you did,' she said. 'And she gave you hand sanitiser for Christmas.'

I tried to put a positive spin on things. 'She's got a really nice house,' I said. 'Everything matches.'

Piper liked matching stuff. She looked thoughtful.

'Will I have my own room?'

I nodded. 'Yes. With cushions on the bed. And potpourri.'

'Really?' Piper perked up. 'I'm not allowed potpourri. It's in case the twins eat it. What's the food like?'

'Good.' I didn't mention the **tiny portions** and **complicated forks**.

Piper shrugged. 'OK. I've got nothing better to do.'

'Do you want to ask your mum?' I said.

'She won't mind,' Piper said. 'She's not like yours, wanting to know where I am, **every second of every day**. She might not notice I've gone.' She sat down on the step. 'Sometimes I wonder if she even likes me.'

'I'm sure she does.' I sat next to her. 'I mean, you're annoying, and your hair's bushy, but mums don't usually mind about things like that.'

'If she liked me,' Piper said, 'she'd let me have a **pet**.'

'Won't she?' I was surprised about that. Even my

mum had agreed to a hamster. 'What did you say you wanted? I mean, if it was a crocodile or—'

'She said "ABSOLUTELY NOT" before I'd even got to that bit.'

'What do you want?' I asked.

'I haven't decided. I just want something. Something that's **mine**.'

'Maybe you should ask when she's in a better mood?' I said.

Piper shook her head. 'She's **NEVER** in a better mood. The twins are up all night.'

I listened to the yelling coming from inside the house.

'How long does it go on for?' I asked.

'Years, probably.' She stood up and pulled something out of her pocket. 'Until then, I'll have to make do with Monty.'

'Who's Monty?' I asked.

'My brother felt sorry for me. **It's his clockwork gerbil.**' She held it out.

It looked a bit moth-eaten. 'It's better than nothing,' I said, kindly.

'Not much,' Piper said.

The next day Mum asked why there was a hazard sticker on Dad's suitcase and wanted to look inside, but he said it would spoil the surprise.

I wondered if I should tell her about the **tigers**. Partly so she wouldn't get eaten, but mostly so she'd refuse to go, and then I wouldn't have to go to Grandma Beatrix's.

I didn't though, as it would spoil things for Dad.

We collected Piper on the way. She climbed in the back next to me and looked around. 'Have you brought Myrtle?' she asked.

I shook my head. 'Grandma Beatrix doesn't like animals,' I said. 'I had to leave her with Mrs Frost next door.'

I'd been worried about Myrtle lately. **She hadn't been herself**. I mean, she is six, which is old for a hamster. Thea Harris, who sits next to me in maths, wasn't very nice about that when I told her. She said that no hamsters live that long, and that Mum must have replaced her, more than once!

I **definitely** don't like Thea as much as I used to.

Mum was looking forward to the holiday so much she didn't seem at all sad to say goodbye. When we got to Grandma's, she practically **pushed** me out of the car! She couldn't wait to get going.

'It's nice to know you'll be well looked after,' she said. 'I've got nothing to worry about.'

I thought about the tigers again.

'I can't believe you've got **wingsuits**.' Piper looked envious. I stepped on her foot. Honestly. I'd told her not to say anything.

'Swimsuits?' Mum said. 'I packed three. That'll be enough, won't it?'

'More than,' Dad said.

Grandma Beatrix looked the same as ever. Her hair was clamped firmly to her head with two metal

19

grips. Even though it was hot, she was wearing a puffy blouse with polka dots, and a woolly suit with **enormous** shoulder pads. She had a badge on her lapel which read *Great Potton Bowls Club, Member of the Year.* There was a lot of air-kissing. She kept saying it had been 'too long' – but it definitely hadn't. Anyone would think I was her favourite grandchild.

I'm not.

My cousin Thomas is definitely her favourite. He has excellent manners and wears waistcoats. I'm pretty sure he knows all of the forks. He's in Russia at the moment, at dance school. He's VERY talented (according to Aunt Sarah).

We waved Mum and Dad off and followed Grandma inside.

'Thanks for inviting me,' Piper said to her. 'Ollie thought he'd get **bored**, but now I'm here, of course he won't be.'

I stepped on Piper's foot. 'I don't remember saying that,' I said. 'I was really looking forward to coming.'

Grandma Beatrix patted her hair. 'I'm so pleased. I know you prefer your other grandma ...' She paused expectantly.

'I like you both the same,' I said, politely.

Grandma Beatrix gave a delighted squeal. 'I'm **SO** glad. In any case, you're going to have a marvellous time. I have some wonderful activities planned.'

'Have you?' I tried to look pleased.

'Oh yes. All sorts of exciting things.' She bustled off along the hall. 'This way.'

Piper smirked.

'What?' I scowled at her.

'Competitive grandparenting,' Piper whispered. 'It's great.'

I blinked. I hadn't heard of competitive grandparenting before. If Grandma Beatrix wanted to beat Grandma Florence, she had quite a lot of ground to make up. I wasn't sure she could do it in a week.

'Who'd like a snack?' Grandma said.

'Ooh, yes, please.' Piper looked thrilled.

We followed Grandma into the dining room. The table was laid with a white cloth and set with **posh china**. It was all very neat and sparkly.

I remembered to pull out Piper's chair for her. She seemed a bit surprised.

'Lovely manners, Ollie.' Grandma gave me an approving nod.

Piper giggled. I ignored her and sat down myself.

Grandma sat down too. She beamed across the table at us. 'I've been thinking,' she said. 'From now on, you can call me **Beatrix**.'

'Just Beatrix?' I said. 'Not Grandma?'

'That's right. Grandma is so ... **STUFFY**.' She unfolded her napkin and tucked it into her puffy blouse. '**Which, of course, I'm not**.'

'OK,' I said. '*Beatrix*.'

Beatrix clapped her hands. 'Wonderful. So much more ... fun, don't you think?'

'Definitely,' I said.

Piper looked around. 'Did you say there were snacks?'

I looked too. There didn't seem to be any. All the plates were empty.

Beatrix wiggled her fingers at us.

Oh.

'We have to wash our hands, Piper.' I got up. 'Come on.'

'For snacks?' Piper looked concerned. 'My mum says we **need** some germs, or we'll die from immunities.'

Beatrix looked stern. 'No washed handies, no biscuits.'

Biscuits?

Blimey.

Grandma Beatrix didn't buy biscuits. She was worse than Mum when it came to trans fats. I cheered up. This must be the competitive grandparenting.

I hoped there were Jaffa Cakes.

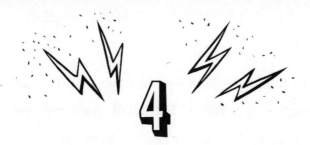

4

As soon as our hands were washed, and we'd sat back down, Beatrix went to get the biscuits.

They were very small biscuits.

They certainly weren't Jaffa Cakes.

They didn't even have chocolate on.

She placed them reverently in front of us.

'They're from Waitrose,' she said.

'Are they?' Piper took two and ate them immediately.

I took one and remembered to nibble it. After each nibble I put it down on the plate and used my napkin to dab my fingers. 'Gracious,' I said. 'These are delicious.'

Beatrix gave me a fond smile. 'Another?'

'Thank you,' I said. 'So kind.'

Piper reached for another one as well.

Grandma whisked the plate away. 'You've had two already, Piper. **Two is sufficient**. We'll save the rest for another day.' She trotted out to the kitchen.

I could see from Piper's face that she didn't think two was sufficient. 'I think I might have to go home,' she whispered. '**I'm starving**.'

'We've only been here five minutes,' I whispered back. 'I'm sure it'll get better.'

Piper didn't look convinced.

Beatrix came back holding a piece of paper. She waved it at us. 'Look,' she said. 'This just came through the door. It seems there's a lovely craft session at the library.' She looked at her watch. 'It starts in twenty minutes. Would you like to go?'

I took the flyer and read it. 'I'm not sure flower pressing is our thing,' I said.

Piper gasped. 'Flower pressing? **I LOVE flower pressing**.' She jumped up. 'Come on, Ollie. It'll be fun.'

I was surprised at Piper, to be honest. I didn't see

her as the flower pressing type. 'I'll go if you want to,' I said.

'Wonderful.' Beatrix pulled open the dresser drawer. 'Now, as it's at the library, I'll pack you some antiseptic wipes.'

'Antiseptic wipes?' Piper looked puzzled. 'What for?'

Beatrix tutted. '**Libraries aren't hygienic**. All those books coming and going. One can never be sure where they've been, can one?'

'Other people's houses?' Piper suggested.

Beatrix gave a shudder. '**Exactly**,' she said.

'Should we take some rubber gloves?' Piper asked. 'Just to be on the safe side?'

Beatrix looked delighted. 'There are some in the kitchen. I'll get them.'

'You never said she was this bad,' Piper hissed.

'Sorry,' I lied. 'I'd forgotten.'

Beatrix came back in with a drawstring bag. 'There you go.' She handed it over. 'Antiseptic

wipes, Marigolds, hand sanitiser and – in case of emergency – disposable loo seat covers.'

'Loo seat covers?'

I gaped at her. Beatrix unrolled one to show us. It looked like a large shower cap with a hole in the middle. 'You pop them on before you sit down,' she said. 'Not, of course, that I have ever used a public lavatory myself.'

'Of course not,' I said.

'Are you happy to walk by yourselves? I have to bake a sponge for the Ladies' Institute Summer Fayre.'

'We'll be fine,' I said.

5

It turned out Piper wasn't interested in flower pressing at all.

'I had to get out,' she said. 'I'm already low on sugar. And immunities. *I could pass out any minute.*'

She said we should have an emergency meeting.

She said if we didn't come up with a plan, she was going home.

I stared at her in horror. 'You can't leave me,' I said.

'I can,' she said.

'She's always bad on the first day,' I lied again. 'Tomorrow she'll be OK.'

'Let's ring your other gran,' Piper said. 'She can rescue us.'

'It's Beatrix's turn,' I said. 'We can't just disappear off.'

Piper shrugged. 'You can't,' she said. 'But I could.'

'It's not that bad,' I said.

Piper looked at me. 'You're holding a bag of toilet seat covers,' she said. **How much worse can it get?'**

•••

Great Potton library wasn't busy. I could see a man with an enormous moustache flicking through a book in the *Wool-craft* section – and some children pulling out CDs – but no one else.

Mrs Hart, the librarian, was sitting at her desk, stamping stuff. We asked her where we should go for the flower pressing, but she said we must have the wrong library.

How odd. The flyer had definitely said it was today. Why would they advertise something that wasn't on?

Piper shrugged. 'Oh well,' she said. 'We may as well stay for a bit. We've got that homework to do on Egypt.'

'I'm going to see if they've got the *Great Potton*

Guardian,' I said. 'Grandma Florence is in it.'

Piper looked thrilled. '**Was she arrested again?**'

'No.' I found the paper on the newspaper rack and spread it out on the table.

It was a good photo. Grandma was holding Rose up to the camera and he had a little medal round his neck.

'Choodles are so cute.' Piper stared at him admiringly. 'Your gran must have done his fur for the photo. Look at his lovely bunches.'

She started to read out the story. 'Ms Brown, thirty-two—'

'**Grandma's not thirty-two!**' I said. '**She's such a liar.**'

'Don't interrupt.' Piper frowned at me.

'Sorry.'

She started again. 'Ms Brown, thirty-two, got more than she bargained for at Lidl last Monday. After hearing a scream from the fruit aisle, her little dog, Rose, sprang from her handbag and dashed to the rescue. Between them, Ms Brown and Rose overpowered an Indian python and removed it to a safe place. Ms Brown said, "I rarely visit the fruit aisle – so thank goodness for Rose."

'A Lidl spokesperson said they had no idea where the snake escaped from.'

'Grandma's bag, probably,' I said.

'I wouldn't be surprised.' Piper folded the paper. 'I wonder what she did with it. **A snake would be a good pet**.'

'Even if your mum changed her mind,' I said, 'she wouldn't be keen on a python. It might swallow the twins.'

I went to put the paper back on the rack. The man with the moustache had moved from *Wool-craft* and was leaning against the wall, flicking through *Caravanning World*. He wasn't reading it, though. **He was peering down one of the aisles**.

I wondered what he was looking at.

I peered down too.

At first, I thought the aisle was empty, but then I noticed someone at the end, lurking in the shadows of *Romance*.

They were wearing a long coat and a large hat with a floppy brim. Sunglasses and a scarf concealed their face.

They looked **suspicious**, if you asked me.

A chill ran down my spine. Mum could be right. Maybe Great Potton was stuffed with kidnappers?

Maybe the man with the moustache was a policeman, staking him out?

I took another look at him.

Oh. Perhaps not. He'd put *Caravanning World* back and was engrossed in *Angler's Monthly*.

When I looked back over to *Romance*, the shadowy figure had gone.

Phew.

I put the paper back and went to find Piper. She was in *Ancient Civilisations*, flicking through books on Egypt.

'What do we need?' she said. *'Mummification for Dummies? A Tale of Tomb Cities?'* She held one out. 'Ollie? Are you listening?'

I wasn't. I was staring over her shoulder as the suspicious figure from Romance emerged from Bulgarian Literature **and shuffled towards us**.

'What are you looking at?' She swung around. 'Oh. Who's that? And why are they wearing that weird hat?'

Now I could see it properly I realised the hat looked exactly like the one Mum had worn to Aunt Sophie's wedding.

The pink feathery one, which had gone missing during the ceilidh.

OMG.

My mouth dropped open.

It WAS Mum's hat.

It wasn't Mum wearing it though.

IT WAS GRANDMA.

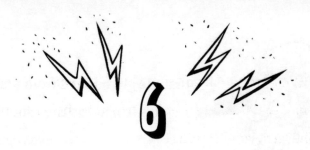

6

WOOHOO!

Grandma took off her sunglasses and looked around furtively. 'Beatrix isn't with you, is she?' she whispered.

'No,' I said. 'She's at home making a cake.'

'Thank **goodness** for that.' Grandma unwrapped her scarf. 'I'm not in need of a lecture at present. I mean, if I was, Beatrix would be the first person I'd look for. But as it happens, I'm not.'

Piper gave her a hug. 'Have you brought Rose?' she asked.

'Of course.' Grandma whipped open her coat. Rose was tucked into the inside pocket.

'He's napping,' Grandma said.

Piper did her usual amount of squealing and woke him up. Rose didn't seem particularly pleased about that. He glared at us from under his fringe and then shut his eyes again.

'He's so cute,' Piper said. 'I'd love a Choodle. I bet if Mum met Rose, she'd let me have one.'

I reminded her that Rose was a **three thousand-year-old Dog of Destiny**, the last of his line, and therefore, **PRICELESS**. 'On your budget,' I said, 'you should probably be thinking about a lizard.'

'I haven't even got enough for that,' Piper said.

Grandma looked thoughtful. 'I may have a spare pet or two at home, Piper. What were you thinking of? A naked mole rat? A tarantula?'

'I need to persuade my mum first,' Piper said. 'Thanks, though.'

'Why are you dressed like that, Grandma?' I asked. 'Aren't you hot?'

'I was in disguise,' Grandma said. 'One has to practise. It's a very useful skill, disguise, and blending in.'

I looked at her bright orange coat. 'Blending into what, exactly?' I said. 'Lava?'

'You never know.' Grandma pulled a packet of custard creams from her pocket. She offered the packet to Piper. 'Biscuit?'

'I don't think we're **supposed** to eat in the library,' I said.

'You sound like Beatrix,' Piper said. She helped herself to three.

Grandma stuffed one in her mouth. 'How is she?'

'**AWFUL**,' Piper said. 'She said two biscuits were sufficient!' She took another. 'And they were tiny.'

Grandma gave her a sympathetic pat. 'Size is very important,' she said. 'Nothing worse than a tiny biscuit.'

'I can't take it much longer,' Piper said.

'I thought you'd like a break,' Grandma said. 'No need to thank me.'

My mouth fell open. 'Did **YOU** put that flower pressing flyer through Beatrix's door?'

'Might have done.' Grandma looked pleased with herself.

Yay!' Piper gave a little hop. 'You're going to rescue us?'

'Oh no.' Grandma shook her head. 'I'm not allowed. Ollie's mum was very clear before she gallivanted off. She said it was Beatrix's turn.'

Piper's face fell. 'So why are we here?'

'Well you're doing Egypt at school, aren't you?' Grandma said. 'I need some help.' She unzipped her bag and started to rummage through it. 'I found something. Well. Rose found it, actually.'

She spent ages looking. Biscuit wrappers flew everywhere.

'Ah. There it is.' She grabbed something from underneath a Wagon Wheel.

She held it out.

'ISN'T IT INCREDIBLE?'

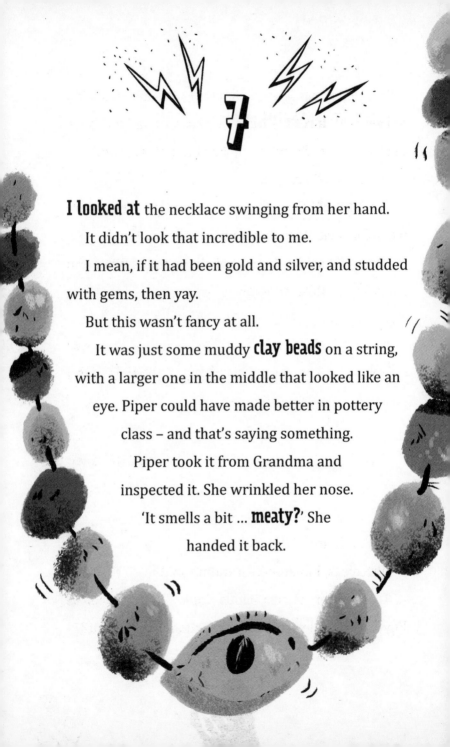

7

I looked at the necklace swinging from her hand.

It didn't look that incredible to me.

I mean, if it had been gold and silver, and studded with gems, then yay.

But this wasn't fancy at all.

It was just some muddy **clay beads** on a string, with a larger one in the middle that looked like an eye. Piper could have made better in pottery class – and that's saying something.

Piper took it from Grandma and inspected it. She wrinkled her nose. 'It smells a bit … **meaty?**' She handed it back.

'It's very old, Piper. **Ancient**. It was probably buried with a rotting corpse. I haven't had a chance to clean it yet.' Grandma flicked off a bit of mud.

'What is it?' I asked.

'An **amulet**,' Grandma said. 'Egyptian. They were worn for luck. Rose dug it up outside my tent.'

'Really?' I said. I thought of all the times Piper and I had taken Rose treasure hunting. He'd never dug anything up for us!

'Yes. I'd pitched it at Great Potton Nature Reserve,' Grandma said. '**I wasn't poaching. Definitely not**. I was um ... badger watching.'

'I love badgers,' Piper said.

'Fascinating creatures,' Grandma agreed. 'Anyway, this morning, I popped Rose outside to do his business, and he came back in with this!'

'Is it valuable?' Piper asked.

'Priceless, I imagine,' Grandma said.

I gave her a suspicious look. 'So a priceless Egyptian amulet was buried outside your tent?' I said. 'And Rose found it, just like that?'

'He's a **lucky** dog, remember.' Grandma lifted Rose out of her coat and gave him a pat, before popping him down on the floor. 'I expect this had lain undisturbed for centuries, just waiting to be found.'

We watched Rose scamper under the checkout desk, where he stopped for a good scratch. Dogs aren't allowed in the library, so it was lucky Mrs Hart had gone over to rearrange *Cakes and Bakes*.

Rose looked quite clean for once.

'You'd think he'd be muddier,' I said. 'All that digging.'

'**What are you trying to say?**' Grandma sounded indignant.

'Nothing,' I said.

'If you are trying to imply that I **stole** the amulet, Ollie, you are quite wrong. **I never steal**.'

'You're banned from Greggs,' I said.

'That was a misunderstanding.' Grandma glared at me. 'Whatever your mother says.'

'You took Rose,' Piper reminded her.

'That was Rose's destiny,' Grandma huffed. 'I had no choice in the matter.'

'If you say so,' I said.

Grandma scowled. '**Do you want to know about the amulet or not?**'

'Sorry,' I said.

Grandma gave me a final glare and carried on. 'Well, I'd just started to clean it, when something amazing happened. Watch.' She pressed the centre of the largest bead.

There was a **CLUNK**, and it split open.

'Blimey,' Piper said. 'Look at that.'

The bead was hollow, like a locket – and inside, there was a **TINY PAPER SCROLL**.

Grandma prised it out and held it up. 'Papyrus. Thousands of years old.'

'Really?' I blinked.

'Absolutely. We need to unlock its secrets.' She unrolled it and placed it reverently on the table.

43

'Don't get crumbs on it.'

The scroll was so small I had to get really close to see anything on it at all. Even then, it just looked like a load of scribble.

'What does it say?' Grandma handed me a magnifying glass. 'Round the edge.'

Even with the glass, the scribble still looked like scribble, just bigger. 'I have no idea,' I said.

Grandma's eyebrows shot up. 'You don't do **hieroglyphs** at Great Potton Primary?'

'No,' I said. 'Just Spanish on a Thursday.'

Grandma tutted. 'What about you, Piper? Are you skilled in ancient language?'

'No.' Piper peered over my shoulder. 'Is that bit in the middle a map?' she said.

'It is.' Grandma nodded. '**A map of Cairo**.'

'Really?' I asked.

'Yes.' Grandma pointed to a blue line. 'This is the Nile. I'd recognise its shape anywhere. And see these little triangles?'

I squinted through the magnifying glass. 'Yes,' I said. 'Those are the pyramids. And look at this!' She stabbed her finger at the grid. 'On the third square in. There's a cross.' She clasped her hands excitedly. 'You know what that means?'

'What?' Piper asked.

'**This is an ancient treasure map**.' Grandma beamed at us.

I stared at her. 'Are you sure?' I said.

'Absolutely,' Grandma said.

'It doesn't look that old.' Piper gave us her opinion. 'And the Nile has definitely been drawn with **felt tip**. It's a very bright blue.'

Grandma scowled. 'This is a **genuine** artefact. If you're going to be like that, don't expect a share of the treasure.' She let the papyrus roll up.

'Are you going to go and look for it?' I asked.

'I certainly am,' Grandma said. 'My hot-air balloon needs fixing and I'm desperately short of cash. A sarcophagus full of treasure is just what I need.'

TREASURE? Suddenly the fact it was Grandma Beatrix's turn didn't seem so important.

'Can we come?' I asked.

'**OMG**.' Piper hopped up and down. 'That'd be fantastic. Even if the map isn't real, I've always wanted to ride a camel. We'd get the best marks ever for our Egyptian homework!'

'The map **IS** real,' Grandma huffed. 'Of course it is.'

'You'll take us, won't you?'

'Sorry.' Grandma shook her head.

'Why not?' I said. 'I need to work on my explorer genes.'

'If you're worried about getting in trouble with Ollie's mum,' Piper said, 'you normally are anyway, so it wouldn't make any difference.'

'I'm not worried about Sukey,' Grandma tutted. 'It's the balloon. It's in a terrible state. The basket is on its last legs. It's fine for me and Rose – but any extra weight ... it could plummet from the sky. **We'd be fish food.**'

Plummeting didn't seem to worry Piper. She carried on trying to persuade Grandma. 'Please let us come,' she said. 'We'll be loads of help.' She picked up the papyrus and squinted at it. 'Look. There's a tiny arrow pointing from the cross ... to a ...' She looked closer. 'A drawing of a cat?' She blinked. 'What does that mean?'

'The whole point of treasure maps, Piper, is that you have to work them out. And that' – Grandma took the scroll back – 'is what I'm going to do. Now.

Where's a dictionary?'

'Excuse me.' The voice came from behind.

I turned around.

It was the man with the moustache.

8

He seemed taller close up. Almost as tall as Grandma. His enormous moustache was silver and matched his wispy hair, which was combed sideways over a large bald patch.

He was very suntanned, which was weird, as the weather hadn't been great recently. He must have been on holiday.

His teeth glinted through his bristles.

I felt a bit uneasy. **Maybe he'd heard us talking about treasure?**

'Hi,' Piper said.

'Can we help you? I asked, politely.

The man completely ignored us! How rude!

He bowed towards Grandma, instead. 'Good afternoon, Madam,' he said.

Grandma eyed him suspiciously. 'Good afternoon.'

'I am so sorry to interrupt,' he said. 'But I was just on my way to check out this book' – he waved a copy of *Crochet Your Christmas Gifts* – 'when I overheard your conversation.' Grandma looked indignant. 'I hope you're not accusing us of being too noisy. We weren't being too noisy. Definitely not. I shushed Ollie at least twice. Shushhhh, Ollie. **Shushhhhh.**'

Piper looked at the man with narrowed eyes. 'Are you a librarian?' she said. 'You can't tell us to be quiet if you're not.'

'No, no.' The man held up his hand. 'You have misunderstood me.'

Grandma looked wary. 'If that's your car parked

outside,' she said, 'the dent in the side had nothing to do with me. **Nothing at all**.'

The man looked bewildered. 'I don't own a car.'

'Oh good.' Grandma looked relieved. 'Because it was a really silly place to park it. Right there, on the road. Anyone could have driven into it. Not that I did – and if I had I'd have owned up right away.'

'It was not my car that you did not hit.' The man held out his hand. 'Allow me to introduce myself. My name is **Geoffrey**. Geoffrey Beaumont. I'm an archaeologist. I specialise in rare Egyptian artefacts.'

Grandma blinked. 'An archaeologist? Gracious. Did you hear that, children? How interesting.'

Geoffrey smoothed back his hair. 'I've been working in Cairo. A wonderful place. Such history. I'm very well respected there.'

Piper looked disbelieving. 'What are you doing here, then?' she asked.

'Visiting a sick aunt. I popped in to collect her

reservation.' He waved the book again. 'I heard you mention Cairo and then ...' He pointed. 'I saw your scroll.'

Grandma hid it behind her back. 'What scroll?' she said.

'The one from the amulet,' Geoffrey said. 'The one you think is a treasure map. Do not worry.' He patted Grandma's arm. 'I'm sure you found it by entirely legitimate means.'

'I certainly did,' Grandma said huffily. 'My dog dug it up.'

'Ah.' Geoffrey's eyes glinted. 'I love little doggies. They make wonderful companions.'

'Rose and I are inseparable,' Grandma said. 'He's a Choodle. Very rare. There have been attempts to steal him recently, so I've attached a tracking device to his collar.' She gave Geoffrey a stern look.

'An unusual name.' Geoffrey peered over at Rose. 'For a male dog.'

'He wasn't called that when we got him,' Piper said.

'He was called Anubis. It was on his collar, wasn't it, Ollie?'

'Was it now?' Geoffrey's eyes gleamed. 'How very interesting.'

Grandma scowled at him. 'What was it you wanted?' she asked.

'Oh yes.' Geoffrey turned back to her. 'The scroll,' he said. 'May I look? I am familiar with hieroglyphics.'

'We're not sharing any treasure,' Piper said. 'Just so you know.'

Geoffrey shook his head. 'I am not interested in riches,' he said. '**Only the mysteries of the past.**' He held out his hand. 'Let me see.'

Grandma didn't seem that keen, but she passed him the scroll. Geoffrey unrolled it and peered closely. '**Aha,**' he muttered to himself. 'Aha, aha, aha.' He tapped the blue squiggle and looked up at Grandma. 'The Nile. You can tell it is the Nile by the distinctive curve, here.' He pointed.

'Is it really?' Grandma said. 'Gracious.'

53

Geoffrey squinted at the triangles. 'The pyramids.' He nodded authoritatively at Grandma. 'Built four thousand years ago by the pharaohs.'

'Is that so?' Grandma sounded a bit testy. 'Who'd have thought?'

Piper giggled. '**He's mansplaining**,' she whispered.

'What's that?' I whispered back.

'It's when a man explains something. Something you already know. You do it all the time, Ollie. It's annoying.'

WHAT A CHEEK! I asked if there was a word for when she explained stuff in her really know-it-all voice – but she smirked and said no, there wasn't.

I said that actually, there was, and it was '*gobby*'.

Then she shoved me, and I fell into the paperback stand and Mrs Hart came over and said could we please be quiet, or she'd ask us to leave.

Geoffrey wasn't taking any notice. He was still studying the map. He tapped the grid and shrugged. He traced the outline of the pyramids. Then he peered closely at the words in Arabic.

He gave a loud gasp.

'I don't believe it,' he whispered. '**BAZ BASARA**.'

9

'Eh?' I said.

'Baz Basara?' Grandma stared at him. 'Who's that?'

Geoffrey looked up at us. His moustache was quivering. 'Baz Basara was an Egyptian chemist. In 3000 BC, he invented a potion. **One that cured all ills**. Boils, snake bites, septic wounds. A reputed potion of life.'

'A potion of life?' Grandma pushed me out of the way so she could peer at the scroll. 'How exciting!'

'Isn't it?' Geoffrey nodded in agreement. 'Traditionally, chemists passed their knowledge to their descendants – but before Baz could do that, there was a terrible incident with a **crocodile**. There wasn't a morsel of him left.'

Grandma gasped. 'The poor man.'

'Indeed.' Geoffrey bowed his head. 'There was a rumour he'd carved the details of the potion into the wall of a tomb. **People searched for years** – but no one ever discovered it.'

'A double tragedy, then.' Grandma shook her head. 'His life's work. Digested.'

Geoffrey's eyes glinted. 'Maybe not. I am wondering if this map shows where the recipe is to be found.'

Grandma stared at him. 'Gracious,' she said. 'That would be **wonderful**.'

'Wouldn't it?' Geoffrey casually twirled his moustache.

Grandma gazed into the distance. 'A potion of life, just waiting to be discovered.'

'A recipe.' Piper sounded disappointed. 'Not treasure.'

'Not gold or silver.' Geoffrey bared his yellowing teeth. 'But just as good.'

Grandma clapped her hands. 'Imagine what we could do with a potion of life! We could set up a pet store. Sell **everlasting hamsters**. Mothers would pay a fortune for those. I'd be able to buy a new balloon!'

'You'd be rich.' Geoffrey nodded in agreement.

'It sounds a bit far-fetched to me.' Piper gave Geoffrey a suspicious look. 'How do you know the map is real?'

'All legends are rooted in truth.' Geoffrey held the papyrus up to the light. He squinted at it. 'This map is **completely** genuine. I'm a respected archaeologist. I should know.'

'But who's going to believe in a potion of life these days?' Piper argued. 'I mean, they might have done in the olden days, when they didn't understand medicine, but they wouldn't now.'

'That's not the point,' Geoffrey looked annoyed. 'Before I became an archaeologist, I obtained a BTEC in business from Great Potton Tech. Even if the potion didn't work, the legend alone would sell it. People would flock from all over Egypt to buy a jar of **Baz Basara's Incredible Life Enhancing Miracle Cream**, whether it worked or not.' He handed the scroll back to Grandma. 'I'm telling you. Everlasting hamsters or face cream. It'd be a money spinner.'

'Gracious.' Grandma looked thrilled.

I wasn't sure about the pet store, or the face cream, but Grandma mentioning hamsters had reminded me of Myrtle.

An ancient potion could be just the thing to sort her out. If it worked, of course.

Grandma clicked open the amulet and popped the scroll back in. 'You're very kind to have enlightened us, Geoffrey,' she said. 'I can't thank you enough.'

'My pleasure.' Geoffrey gave Grandma another bow, then reached into his pocket. He pulled out a small card. 'Here's my number in Cairo. If you come to search for the tomb – you must call me. I will help all I can. Au revoir.' He headed for the door.

'What a **delightful** man.' Grandma beamed after

him, then turned back to us. 'There'll be none of that Baz's Miracle Cream nonsense, though. **Florence's Fabulous Face Cream Number Two** sounds far better.' She gazed into the distance. 'I can see the bottles now. Cut glass. All lined up with fancy labels.'

'You could have your picture on them,' Piper said.

Grandma thought that was an excellent idea. 'I'll set up a stall at Great Potton Market. I'll make a fortune.'

'I didn't think you cared about money,' I said. 'Just rare stuff.'

'I don't normally,' Grandma said, 'but when I took my balloon to the garage, they said it would cost three thousand pounds to fix.'

'**Three thousand pounds?** That's loads.' Piper looked horrified.

'What's wrong with it?' I said.

'It needs a new basket. Remember the hole?'

'Where the rhino stepped on it?'

'Yes. It's getting bigger. Things keep falling

through,' Grandma explained. 'I almost lost Rose the other day. Your mum would have a fit if she saw it, Ollie.'

Mum would have a fit. **Even if it wasn't broken**.

She doesn't know Grandma's balloon has an engine. Which means she doesn't know it goes a **million times** faster than regular hot-air balloons, either.

She wouldn't approve.

10

Mrs Hart had finished rearranging *Cakes and Bakes* and was heading back to *Check-out*. I went to get Rose, before she noticed him. I popped him into the bag of wipes Beatrix had given us, though I didn't do up the drawstring.

Piper was still trying to get Grandma to take us with her.

'We don't **have** to go in your balloon. We could get a regular plane,' she said.

Grandma shook her head. 'There'll be too many officials at the airport, making a fuss about dog germs. The balloon will be fine if it's just Rose and me. I'll leave this evening. If we don't crash, we should be in Cairo by daybreak.'

Rose stuck his head out of the bag. He gave a sharp yap.

Then he started to struggle.

Piper stopped arguing. 'What's wrong with him?' she said.

What *was* wrong with Rose? **He'd gone completely crazy!** I couldn't hold him. He was yipping and snapping, and all his hair was on end.

He sprang out of the bag and raced under *Crime*.

'Gracious. Look at his lovely ruff,' Grandma said. 'Where did he get that?'

'It's a loo seat cover,' Piper said.

'So dashing.' Grandma looked over fondly. 'Have you got any more?'

'Loads.' Piper handed her the bag.

I knelt down and peered under the bookshelf.

'Do you think he saw a mouse?' Piper said.

'Maybe.' Rose likes small furry things. He's tried to eat Myrtle more than once.

'Ollie.' Piper tapped me with her foot. 'Mrs Hart is looking. I think she heard the yapping.'

Mum would be cross if we got banned from the library. **I HAD TO GET ROSE OUT, AND QUICKLY.** I threw myself on to my stomach.

'See if you can reach him with my selfie stick.' Grandma pulled one from her bag.

'Thanks.' I took it.

Rose was as far away as he could get. I inched under the shelf. The loo seat cover was his downfall. It gave me something to hook.

'**GOT HIM,**' I said.

Piper seized my ankles and dragged me out. Rose was scrabbling and yipping. He even tried to bite me with his tiny little teeth. I handed him to Grandma.

She popped him into her handbag and zipped it up.

'There's biscuits in there,' she said. 'He'll soon

calm down.'

'Excuse me?' Mrs Hart called from the desk. 'What's going on?'

'Nothing.' Grandma gave her a cheery wave. 'You may have **thought** you heard a dog, but you **definitely didn't**.' She pushed us toward the exit. 'Though do check for rodents,' she called over her shoulder. 'We saw a mouse. It ran over there.'

Mrs Hart stood up in horror.

Grandma bundled us out.

'**Oh no**.' Piper stopped dead.

I bumped into her. 'What?'

'**IT'S BEATRIX**.' She pointed down the street.

Piper was right. There she was, marching through the shoppers. Grandma wrapped her scarf around her face and legged it. She disappeared around the corner just as Beatrix flapped up beside us.

'I thought I'd come to meet you while the cake was cooling,' she said. 'How was the flower pressing?'

'Brilliant.' I said. 'Such fun.'

'We did some homework as well,' Piper said. 'On Egypt.'

I saw Beatrix's face. 'Don't worry,' I said. 'We used the wipes.'

Beatrix looked relieved. 'I must have a word with the council. E-books are so much more hygienic—' She suddenly stopped and stared up the street. **'Is that Florence's Mini?'** she said.

Grandma's car shot past us.

'No,' I said. 'Hers is orange.'

'That **was** orange.'

'It wasn't,' Piper said. 'It was green.'

'Yep. It was green, Beatrix,' I said. I gave her a little pat on the arm.

Beatrix blinked. 'I could have **sworn** it was orange,' she muttered. She gave herself a shake. 'No matter.'

'Easy mistake,' I said.

'You're right.' She looked at her watch. 'Well, it's not quite teatime, so as a special treat, I'll take you to the park.'

'Great Potton Park?' Piper raised her eyebrows. 'That'll be great, because we *never* go there.'

I nudged her. It would be better than going back to Beatrix's.

'I hope it's improved,' Beatrix said. 'Last time I went ...' She looked around and dropped her voice to a whisper. 'There was a drawing on the bandstand.'

'A drawing of what?' Piper looked interested.

Beatrix shuddered. 'Nothing you need to know about, Piper. I wrote to the council immediately. They said they'd deal with it.'

'Phew,' I said. 'That's a relief.'

'Isn't it?' Beatrix said. 'And I've brought some disinfectant spray for the swings, just in case.'

11

'I cannot believe your gran is off to Cairo and we're stuck here,' Piper muttered. 'I didn't even get time to go and see the drawing.'

We were on our way back to Beatrix's.

We'd only been in the park five minutes. Then a boy next to me on the roundabout had scratched his head.

Beatrix had raced over.

'NITS,' she'd hissed. 'TIME TO GO.'

Now she was bustling along in front of us. 'There's no need to worry,' she called over her shoulder. 'I've got plenty of lotion and a special comb back at the house.'

I was just about to tell her how pleased I was about that, when I heard her phone ping. She looked at it and stopped. 'My goodness,' she said.

'Is everything all right?' I caught up with her.

'Oh yes.' Beatrix sounded thrilled. 'We have a visitor for tea.'

'Who?' I asked.

'One of my *favourite* people.'

I closed my eyes.

It was going to be the vicar, wasn't it?

If it wasn't the vicar, it might be Mrs Eggleton-Cox, who runs the Ladies' Institute. If it was her, I'd have to do the swan thing with the napkins again.

If I had to do the swan thing, Piper would mock me.

Of course, it could be Betty, Beatrix's next-door neighbour. She often pops over to talk about her bowels.

•••

It turned out not to be the vicar. It wasn't the vicar, it wasn't Mrs Eggleton-Cox, and it wasn't Betty.

It was Thomas.

WOO HOO!

Cousin Thomas.

There he stood in his **little pink waistcoat**.

I've never been so pleased to see anybody.

'Hi, Ollie,' he said. He held out his hand. *Fabulous* to see you.'

'Aren't you supposed to be in Russia?' I asked.

'Did you get expelled, Thomas?' Piper gave him a hug.

'No.' Thomas hugged her back. 'I'm over for the Great Potton Festival of Contemporary Dance. I was chosen to represent the school. It's a great honour.' He gave a twirl. 'I'll show you my costume.' He went and got it. It was very feathery. He even had a crown. He put it on to show us. 'Cool,' Piper said. I said I thought it was cool too, even though I didn't.

'Thomas is doing very well,' Beatrix said. 'Sarah said his dance is by far the most **original**.' She gave Thomas a proud pat. 'He's the favourite to win.'

Thomas blushed. 'I did work quite hard on it. Would you like to see?'

Beatrix seemed keen. She went to find her iPod while Thomas curled up in a little feathery ball in the centre of the room.

In my experience, the music he dances to sounds like someone's stepped on a cat. Today was no exception. It started with its usual S C R E E C H.

Thomas unfurled himself and raised his arms.

He stood motionless for a second or two.

Then he leapt into the air, making grabbing motions, with an expression of fear on his face.

He fell to the floor before rising to his knees and swaying backwards and forwards with his eyes shut.

He was there for so long I thought he might have finished, but he hadn't.

He jumped to his feet and started to spin.

'Isn't he wonderful?' marvelled Beatrix, as he **pirouetted** by.

'Exceptional.' His foot had just missed my head.

Thomas disappeared into the hallway.

There was a crash, and a pause, before he *can-canned* back into the room.

'If I win,' he told us, between kicks, 'I'll get a solo in the next big production.'

Feathers flying, he did a final twirl, somersaulted over the dining table and crumpled into a corner.

BLIMEY.

'Was that meant to happen?' Piper whispered.

Beatrix clapped vigorously. 'What a talent.' She dabbed away a tear (of joy, I think).

Thomas stood up and took a bow, beaming. 'It's called *Cherry Picking in the Spring*,' he said. 'It's a metaphor for oppression in the workplace.'

'Wonderful.' Beatrix kept clapping. 'We'll come and watch you.'

'I'd love that.' Thomas looked delighted. 'It's not till

next Saturday. You can help me practise. I'm thinking of doing it blindfolded for added drama.'

I wondered if I could ask to be blindfolded too.

'I've invited Thomas to stay with us,' Beatrix said. 'I thought he might as well, as you two are here.'

Yay! Things were looking up. If Beatrix was busy cooing over Thomas all week, she'd have less time to lecture me and Piper.

I was just about to tell him how pleased I was, when his phone rang. He looked at the screen. 'It's my dance teacher,' he said. 'He's still at the rehearsals. I'd better take it.' He went out into the hall.

When he came back, he looked horribly miserable.

'What's wrong?' I asked.

Thomas looked like he was going to cry. 'It's Xavier, the French competitor.'

'What about him? Piper asked.

'**His dance is almost identical to mine**.' Thomas took off his crown and looked at it sadly. 'Even his costume is the same.' His face crumpled. 'He's on before me. My performance won't have the same impact now.'

Piper got him a tissue. 'I bet he can't jump as high as you. Your grabbing was **superb**.'

'I thought the end was brilliant.' I offered him a biscuit.

Thomas took one and munched on it mournfully. 'I'll have to think of something else. I've got a week.'

Beatrix gave him a sympathetic pat. 'Just watch those crumbs, dear.' She went to get her dustpan.

'We'll help, Thomas,' Piper said. 'Ollie and I are great at thinking of things, aren't we, Ollie?' She gave me a kick.

'Yes,' I said. 'Very good.'

'And we'll help you find a new costume.'

'Really?' Thomas cheered up. 'That would be very kind of you.'

'Ollie,' Beatrix called from the kitchen. 'I just heard the doorbell. Would you get it for me?'

'Of course, Beatrix,' I called back.

I hoped it wasn't the vicar.

It wasn't.

It was Grandma.

She was wearing a disposable loo seat cover around her neck and was holding a cake.

It looked very much like the cake that Beatrix had baked for the Ladies' Institute Summer Fayre.

It **couldn't** be though, as I'd seen Beatrix's cake in the kitchen just a minute ago, where she'd left it to cool by an open window.

'What are you doing here?' I said.

'Needs must.' Grandma marched past me up the hall.

'Eh?' I followed her into the dining room.

'Afternoon, Beatrix,' Grandma said. 'So lovely of you to invite me to tea. I've brought a cake.' She plonked it on the table.

Beatrix seemed quite surprised to see Grandma. She dropped her little dustpan and stood there with her mouth open.

Then she remembered her manners. 'I'm so glad you could make it, Florence,' she said. 'Do sit down.'

Grandma already had. She pulled the teapot towards her and poured herself a cup. Then she cut a slice of cake.

'Anyone else?' she said with her mouth full.

'Yes please.' Piper rushed over. 'It looks lovely. Did you make it?'

'**I did**.' Grandma took another bite. 'Just this morning. It's delicious, even if I say so myself.'

Beatrix's mouth fell open again.

'I kept tight hold of it all the way here.' Grandma waved the knife. 'I heard that there's a cake thief about. I didn't want anyone to steal it, having put so much effort into making it.'

'It looks glorious,' Thomas said. 'Is it lemon?'

'Oh no,' Grandma said. '**I'd never put fruit in a cake**.'

'It tastes like lemon,' Piper said.

'Oh well. Maybe I did.' Grandma shrugged.

77

'If you made it' – Beatrix looked icy – 'surely you'd know?'

'Now you come to mention it ...' Grandma brushed crumbs off her top. 'I clearly remember putting a lemon in. **Two**, in fact.'

'It's very nice,' Thomas said. 'I didn't realise you could bake, Florence.'

'**I made that cake**,' Beatrix said, in fury. '**I left it in the kitchen to cool**.'

'It couldn't have been this cake,' Grandma said. 'I made this one. Yours must have been stolen.'

'I made it for the Ladies' Institute Summer Fayre.' Beatrix was purple.

'The Ladies' Institute?' Grandma looked up from her plate. 'I bumped into the chairperson on the way here. Mrs Eggleton-Cox. She said she's resigning.'

That stopped Beatrix in her tracks. She blinked. '**RESIGNING?**'

'That's right.' Grandma nodded. 'She couldn't decide who to nominate for the role. You, or Mary from the newsagents. She's going to decide this evening.'

Beatrix forgot about the cake. 'Gracious.' She grabbed a bunch of sweet peas from a vase on the windowsill. 'That's a big decision. I might pop over and see if she needs any help.'

'I'm sure she'd appreciate it.' Grandma gave a wave. 'I'll keep an eye on the children.'

'If you're sure?' Beatrix was already on her way out the door.

It **SLAMMED** behind her.

13

'Right.' Grandma sprang to her feet. 'All hands on deck.'

'Are we going boating?' Thomas looked excited.

'No.' Grandma crammed the last of the cake into her mouth and grabbed her bag. 'It's Rose. I was in the park, all set to take off, and he scarpered. I couldn't catch him. **I need your help**.'

'You didn't need our help earlier,' Piper said. 'When we **offered** to come with you.'

'Well, I do **now**.' Grandma headed for the door. 'Quick, before the old bat gets back. We can use my app to track him.'

The park wasn't far. Grandma's balloon was tethered in the corner, bobbing in the breeze. She raced ahead of us, holding up her phone. A red dot flashed on the screen.

'He's in that flower bed.' She pointed. 'Get ready to grab him.'

She **launched** herself in the air.

She managed to flatten a whole load of geraniums, but Rose didn't run out.

Grandma sat up and waved something. It was Rose's collar. The tracking device swung from it. 'The naughty dog. **He's slipped it.**'

Piper looked around. 'So where's he gone?'

Grandma stood up. 'It's not like him to run off. He can't have gone far.'

'How about the bandstand?' Thomas headed off up the hill.

Piper followed him. 'I'll check the drawing's been cleaned off,' she said. 'I'm sure Beatrix would like to know.'

'Any sign?' Grandma called after them. She seemed anxious. It wasn't like her. **Grandma never worried about anything.** 'He's behaved strangely since we were in the library,' she said. 'Something's wrong, but

81

I don't know what.'

'He did seem spooked,' I said.

'Do you think it was the mouse?'

I shook my head. 'We didn't actually see a mouse. It was when you talked about going to Cairo. Maybe ...'

I stopped. I didn't want to say it.

'Maybe what?' Grandma looked at me.

'Well. He's **supposed** to be a teller of fortune, isn't he?'

'Yes.'

'He might be trying to **stop** you going,' I said.

'Why?' Grandma looked surprised. 'He loves going in my balloon.'

I shrugged. 'Perhaps he knows something you don't?' I said. 'Perhaps you're going to crash, or ... or ... **be eaten by a crocodile?**'

Grandma patted me on the shoulder. 'Don't be silly, Ollie. Rose is a bringer of luck. Nothing like that is going to happen.'

'It was just a thought,' I said.

It was a thought that made me nervous.

Thomas waved at us from the bandstand. 'He's under here,' he called. 'Though he won't come out.'

We sped up.

'Rose?' Grandma knelt down. 'Don't be difficult. We need to get going.'

'It's a shame you didn't bring Myrtle,' Piper said to me. 'We could have used her for bait.'

'Ha,' I said. 'Funny.'

'OMG.' Piper stopped dead. '**We can use Monty**.' She reached into her pocket and pulled out her brother's clockwork gerbil. She held it out. 'Here you go.'

'Brilliant.' I took it from her and wound it up.

Then I put it down.

It shot off at speed.

Rose couldn't resist. He **tore** out from under the bandstand.

Thomas was waiting. He flew through the air and rugby-tackled Rose into a bed of petunias. 'Got him,' he yelled.

83

We ran over to help.

'Hold him while I put his collar back on,' Grandma said.

Rose wasn't very keen. He **snarled** and **snapped**, and then he got hold of the collar with his tiny little teeth and shook it like a rat.

By the time Grandma got it out of his jaws, the tracker had gone.

'Oh dear.' She peered into his mouth. '**I think he's swallowed it**.'

'I wouldn't worry,' Piper said. 'My brother's always doing that with Lego. You get it back in the end.'

I didn't ask how.

It wasn't easy, but we finally got Rose into Grandma's bag.

'He'll be fine when we get to Cairo.' Grandma zipped it up. 'I expect he needs a bit of sun.'

Rose **YAPPED** loudly.

'I still don't think he wants to go,' I said.

'You could leave him with us,' Piper said.

Grandma looked indignant. 'Have you seen my balloon? **I need all the luck I can get**.'

'Well, if you won't leave him,' Piper said, 'you'll have to take one of us. Suppose he escapes again?'

Thomas's hand shot up. 'I'm happy to volunteer.'

Piper gave him a shove. 'You've got to rehearse. I'll go.'

'**I'll go**,' I said. 'I need to work on my explorer genes. And she's **my** grandma.'

We glowered at each other.

85

Grandma started walking towards the balloon. 'I'll think about it while I'm untying the ropes,' she said.

I raced after her. '**I'll** do the ropes, Grandma.'

'**I will.**' Piper caught me up.

Thomas shot past us. '**Already** doing it,' he yelled.

I sped up. I wasn't going to let him get there before me.

'Tell you what,' Grandma said. 'Take one each. The first person to undo theirs comes to Cairo.'

'Great idea, Ollie's gran.' Piper tried to trip me, but I dodged her.

I got to the balloon before them and chose the easiest-looking knot.

Grandma climbed into the balloon. 'All set?' she bellowed. '**GO.**'

I'm a scout. I was going to win this if it killed me.

I reached fo—

'**Finished!**' Piper shouted.

Eh? She must have cheated. I turned to complain. Too late.

She was already in the basket. She looked thrilled. **Yay**,' she said. 'I'm off to Cairo.' She gave a little hop. 'Bye, you two.'

The basket gave a creak.

'Less of the hopping,' Grandma ordered. 'In fact, if you could not move at all, that would be good.'

Blimey. I hadn't realised the basket was that bad. There were holes all over it. Even so. I still wanted to go. She was **my** grandma and Piper was going to have all the fun!

I finished untying my rope in a huff.

Piper called to me.

I ignored her. I expect she wanted to gloat.

'**Ollie!**' she said again.

'What?' I scowled at her.

She pointed towards the park gates. '**It's Beatrix!**'

14

'She looks cross,' Grandma said. 'We better hide.' She pulled me in to the basket. 'Get under this.' She threw me a duvet.

Thomas was still untying his rope.

I leant over the side. 'Thomas,' I hissed. 'It's Beatrix.'

'Oh, OK.' He scrambled in.

'I wonder how she knew we were here?' Grandma tutted.

Piper looked up at the balloon. 'I can't imagine,' she said.

Then she said, '**Why are we going up?**'

'We're not going up,' Grandma said. 'We're still tethered.'

I looked through a hole in the basket. The ground was definitely moving away from us. 'We're not.'

Grandma blinked. 'Did someone untie the fourth rope?'

'Oh.' Thomas looked surprised. 'Were we not supposed to?'

'No,' Grandma said.

'**Oops**,' Thomas said.

Grandma blinked. 'Never mind,' she said. 'The basket seems to be holding.' She stood up and waved down at Beatrix. 'Sorry,' she called. '**It was Thomas's fault**.'

'Sorry, Beatrix.' Thomas hung over the side apologetically.

'Florence?' Beatrix's voice drifted up. 'You bring Ollie back right this minute. It's **my** turn. We're going to do colouring tomorrow. I went to Hobby-land especially.'

I felt bad.

It wasn't that I wanted to do colouring in. I wanted to go to Cairo with Grandma, **more than anything**. But Beatrix was right. It **was** her turn.

'Grandma,' I said. 'You better land.'

'Do I have to?' Grandma said. 'Beatrix will shout at me.'

'Yes,' I said. 'You do.'

'OK.' Grandma looked sulky, but she let some of the air out of the balloon.

We started to drift back down.

'I'm **still** going to Cairo.' Piper glared at me.

'Whatever,' I said. **I felt really miserable**. My phone buzzed. It was probably a text from Beatrix, starting her telling-off already. I pulled it out of my pocket and looked at it.

It wasn't from Beatrix. It was from Mrs Frost.

OH NO.

Piper saw my face. 'What's wrong?' she said.

'It's Myrtle,' I said. 'Mrs Frost says she's really sick.'

'Well, she's nearly seven,' Piper said, kindly. 'Maybe it's her time?'

'No.' I shook my head. It wasn't Myrtle's time. 'Go back up, Grandma,' I said. 'We need to go to Cairo and bring back the potion of life. It's Myrtle's only chance.'

'I'm on it, Ollie.' Grandma gave the burner rope an almighty tug.

Up we shot.

I leant over the side of the balloon. Beatrix looked very small.

'**Sorry**,' I shouted. '**I really am**.'

15

We were over Basingstoke when Thomas saw the sea. He gave a *battement* of joy.

He probably shouldn't have done.

The basket **creaked**, and some of the strands holding the bottom to the sides **SNAPPED**.

Thomas grabbed a rope to steady himself.

It didn't help that it was the burner rope. **The basket rocked and shot up again.**

'Whoa.' Piper grabbed Grandma's bag, which was sliding towards the gap. 'We almost lost Rose.'

'Is he all right?' I asked. 'You better have a look.'

Piper undid the zip. Rose stuck his head out and yapped furiously. He didn't look very pleased.

'I'm not a fan of rules.' Grandma looked at Thomas. 'But I think, given the circumstances, it would be **sensible** for me to ban dancing in the basket.'

I stared at her in horror. I'd never heard Grandma use the word 'sensible' before.

It made me worry.

So did the state of the basket. The floor was barely attached to the sides. Grandma suggested we should all sit on the rim, so if the bottom dropped out completely, we wouldn't go with it.

'I'm about to start the engine,' she said. **Hold tight.**

There was a lurch as the balloon picked up speed.

The floor dropped another few centimetres.

'**Blimey.**' Even Piper looked pale.

'Don't panic,' Grandma reassured us. 'I'm **sure** it'll last till we get there.'

The basket gave another lurch. I stared down at the sea. **It was very big.** I mean, I had my fifty-metre badge, but if we crashed I wasn't sure fifty metres would be enough.

'How long until we're over land?' I asked.

Grandma didn't reply. She was looking over her

93

shoulder, in the direction we'd come from. 'Gracious,' she said. 'How strange.'

'What?' I asked.

She ignored me. She pulled a spyglass from her coat pocket and put it to her eye. 'It's a plane,' she muttered.

A plane?

She handed me the spyglass.

I put it to my eye.

Blimey.

It was a plane. A small one, a bit like Dad's.

It seemed to be heading straight for us.

Well. Not quite straight for us. Every now and then it'd drop slightly, and then it would do a loop the loop. Whoever was in it didn't seem to be very good at flying.

I gave the spyglass to Piper, so she could see.

'Grandma?' I said.

'Yes, dear?'

Is anyone after you?

Grandma looked indignant. 'Like who?'

'The person the amulet belongs to?' I suggested.

'The amulet belongs to me, Ollie.' Grandma looked outraged. 'I told you. Rose dug it up.'

'Maybe Geoffrey told someone about it?' Piper suggested. 'A potion of life is probably quite sought after.'

That's all we needed. Someone else after the recipe. We had to get there first. **We needed the potion for Myrtle!**

The plane was getting closer.

Grandma went over to the engine. 'I'll turn this off and fire up the burners. We'll shoot up into the clouds. I'm sure they're not interested in us, but just in case.'

It sounded like a good plan.

It wasn't.

When Grandma turned the engine off we didn't go up. We started going down.

'What's wrong?' I started to panic.

'Nothing to worry about.' Grandma thumped a dial. 'The burners aren't working. We're out of gas. There must be a leak.'

Nothing to worry about? The plane was so close I could practically see into the cockpit.

'Oh dear.' Thomas looked anxious. 'I hope they know how to stop.'

'It doesn't look like it.' Piper made a grab for Rose.

'**BRACE FOR IMPACT!**' shouted Grandma.

I clung on to the edge as tightly as I could and shut my eyes. Mum was going to go mad when she found out about—

'Ollie?'

It was Piper. She was shaking my arm.

I opened an eye.

Oh. We were still in one piece. The plane must have done a last-minute swerve.

There it was, in the distance. I stared after it.

'See?' Grandma sounded triumphant. 'Nothing to do with the amulet. Just someone out on a jolly.'

'If you say so,' I said. I peered over the edge of the basket. The sea was looking closer.

'We need to gain height,' Grandma said. 'Throw everything out.'

We looked, but apart from the flowery duvet, and Grandma's bag with Rose in it, there wasn't anything to throw out.

Grandma shrugged. 'We'll have to land,' she said.

'Land?' I stared at her in horror. **'In the sea?'**

'Don't be silly,' Grandma said. 'We'd be eaten by sharks.'

'Where, then?'

'On that cruise ship,' Grandma said. 'See it?' She pointed. 'You'll have to direct me. If we're out by a centimetre we're in trouble.'

'Are we landing on the deck?' Thomas craned his neck.

'Yes. In their swimming pool.' Grandma switched off the sat nav and took the rudder.

There it was. **A tiny square of blue**.

Piper hung over the edge. '**Down a bit**.'

'**Right a bit**,' Thomas shouted.

'**Left a bit**.'

'**MAINTAIN DESCENT**.'

We were getting closer. We'd definitely been spotted. People were climbing off their sun loungers and pointing.

'Your mum's not on a cruise, is she?' Piper asked.

'No.'

'That's good.'

'Evacuate the pool,' Grandma bellowed.

Everyone scattered.

SPLASH.

We were down.

Grandma hopped out of the basket. She dragged Thomas with her.

'I've brought the **dance act** for tonight,' she announced. 'He missed his flight and was so worried you'd be disappointed.'

Everyone clapped.

Thomas curtseyed and did something with his arms.

Everybody clapped again.

'Where's the captain?' Grandma looked around. 'I'll go and have a word.'

•••

The captain didn't look particularly pleased about the balloon in his pool, to be honest.

He muttered a lot about the good old days and something called a '**brig**'.

I didn't know what a brig was, so Piper explained it was something pirates locked people up in before making them walk the plank.

The captain said that, sadly, due to regulations, walking the plank wasn't an option either, so we better get our passports, and go and sit in the lounge until we docked.

I looked at Grandma.

Passports?

We didn't have passports. How could we? We'd been in the park before taking off, with no access to paperwork.

'No need to worry, Ollie.' Grandma waved a card at me.

It was the one Geoffrey had given her in the library.

'I'll call him,' she said. 'When I tell him about our passports tumbling into the sea, I'm sure he'll be able to help.'

'But they didn't.' Thomas looked puzzled.

'Didn't what?' Grandma raised her eyebrows.

'Tumble into the sea.'

'**Yes**, they did.' Grandma nodded earnestly. 'We all had our passports; they were in a little velvet bag. The balloon gave a lurch, and they fell out. Somewhere near Italy, I think.'

'Did they?' Thomas looked very surprised. 'But mine is back in Great Potton, in my suit—'

Piper gave him a nudge. 'Thomas,' she said. 'I saw the little velvet bag with my very own eyes. I tried to grab it – but I wasn't in time.'

'It was **terrible** luck,' Grandma said. 'I watched them plummet.'

'All the way down,' I said. '**Splash**.'

'Oh.' Thomas finally understood. '**THAT** bag.'

'A shame,' Piper said. 'It was so pretty.'

'Wasn't it?' Thomas agreed.

Grandma went to find a signal, so she could call Geoffrey – and we went to find Rose, who'd run off again. He was under a lifeboat. Piper still had Monty the clockwork gerbil, so we tempted him out with that.

Rose wasn't best pleased when Thomas leapt on him again. I held open Grandma's bag and together we managed to stuff him in. 'Come on,' I said. 'We'll be in Cairo by the morning. Please cheer up.'

Rose gave a whimper. He burrowed into the bottom and lay still. I offered him a custard cream, but he just hid his head under his paws.

'Do you think he's OK?' Thomas looked worried.

I shrugged. 'I don't know.' I hoped he wasn't ill, like Myrtle.

Poor Myrtle. The thought of her, hundreds of miles away, all sick and alone, made my insides ache. I hoped Mrs Frost had fluffed up her bedding enough. I stared over the rail at the distant shore. **The sooner we found that recipe, the better**. I just hoped we had enough time. 'We should get back to Grandma,' I said. 'I hope she got hold of Geoffrey.'

We found Grandma up on the top deck. She was putting her phone away.

103

'He was thrilled to hear from me,' she said. 'Over the moon.'

'Did you tell him about the velvet bag?' Thomas asked.

'Oh yes. He was ever so sympathetic. He's out of town at the moment, but he's spoken to a friend of his, who works at the town hall. Her name's Cleo. **Cleo Rafarty**. Geoffrey said she was most excited to hear about the amulet. She loves a good treasure hunt. She's sending a car for us.'

'Really?' Piper looked concerned. 'Can you trust her? Suppose she steals the map?'

Grandma gave her a pat. 'Egypt is full of proper treasure. She wouldn't be interested in an old recipe.'

The captain shouted something about the balloon as we walked down the gangplank. Grandma gave him a friendly wave. 'We'll collect it later,' she called. 'Thank you so much.'

He didn't look very happy.

Grandma bustled ahead. 'There's the car. Black with a flag on it. Just like Geoffrey said.'

The driver got out to open the back door for us. 'Welcome,' he said. His teeth glinted in the sun. 'Four of you and a leetle doggy? Is that right?'

'It certainly is,' Grandma said. 'We're off to the town hall. We found an amu—'

'Shall we get going?' I interrupted. As far as I was concerned, the fewer people who knew about our map, the better.

I climbed into the back and the others scrambled in after me. Piper sat and looked around admiringly. 'It's very posh,' she said. 'Cleo must have a lot of money.'

'Geoffrey said she was successful,' Grandma agreed.

The driver said he'd take us the quickest way, but Cairo was ever so busy. There was **loads** of traffic which barely moved, and when it did, there didn't seem to be any rules. Cars and lorries and tuk-tuks went around roundabouts whichever way they felt like, loudly beeping their horns. I kept checking on Rose to make sure he was OK, but he just lay in Grandma's bag looking miserable. I really hoped he wasn't ill. **Maybe we should find him a vet?**

•••

At last, the driver pointed ahead. 'Cairo Town Hall,'

he said. 'I vill radio Cleo and let her know you have arrived.'

'Gracious.' Grandma peered out of the window as we cruised through enormous gilded gates. **Isn't it grand?**

It was. Two huge pillars stood either side of great stone steps, which led to a very fancy door. It didn't look like the sort of town hall you'd hire for a jumble sale, or a disco party.

Wow, Piper said. 'It's **SO** cool.'

'It looks really old,' I said.

'Ancient civilisations were so refined,' Grandma said, admiringly.

'Apart from the slaves, and fly swatters made from giraffe tails,' Piper said.

'Apart from those,' Grandma agreed.

As we clambered out of the car, the door above us flew open.

The woman who stood at the top of the steps was about the same age as Grandma, but her hair was curled into shiny black sausages and piled on top of her head. Her suit had even **bigger** shoulder pads than Beatrix's, which I hadn't thought was possible.

'That must be **Cleo**,' Grandma said.

'Look at her shoes.' Thomas blinked. 'They're amazing.'

They were. They were ever so high. And glittery.

They sparkled in the sun.

As did all the gold around her neck.

'She's very bling,' said Piper.

'She's head of tourism.' Grandma gave her a wave. 'She knows **everything** there is to know about Ancient Egypt. She's a very good friend of Geoffrey's.'

Cleo tottered down the steps. 'Florence?' She held out a ringed hand.

Grandma shook it. 'Lovely to meet you, Cleo,' she said.

'Charmed to meet you too, Florence.' Cleo bared her sparkling white teeth. 'Geoffrey told me about your discovery. Quite remarkable.' She stooped and peered into the car we'd just got out of. 'Just the four of you?' she enquired.

'That's right,' Grandma said. 'Ollie, Piper and Thomas. **They're here to help**.'

'Geoffrey said you'd be bringing a doggy? I do love doggies.'

'Oh yes.' Grandma pointed at her bag, which I was still holding. 'Rose is in there. He's a bit out of sorts at the moment, so we've left him to sleep.'

'You must let me see.' Cleo teetered over and held her arms out for the bag. I didn't feel like giving it to her, to be honest. Suppose Rose dashed off again?

I didn't have much choice, though. **She**

snatched it.

'I'm worried about him,' I said. 'He's not himself.'

'Let me see.' She unzipped the bag and peered inside. '**Wonderful.**' She seemed thrilled. 'Geoffrey was right. It **is** a Choodle. What an adorable little thing.'

Grandma looked proud. 'They're very rare.'

'They are indeed.' Cleo was quite overcome. 'Such a **handsome** chap.' She zipped up the bag and slung it across her shoulder.

I thought that was a bit much, seeing as it was Grandma's bag!

'Is he all right?' I asked.

'Just a teeny bit off colour.' Cleo turned and clopped up the steps. 'I know an excellent vet. I'll call him the minute we're inside.'

Grandma clasped her hands. 'Thank you. Rose is so dear to me. I couldn't **bear** it if anything happened to him.'

'I can see why.' Cleo patted the bag. 'He's such a sweetheart.'

110

'I **love** your shoes.' Thomas skipped alongside her.

'How kind.' Cleo beamed at him. 'I had them made. They were **terribly** expensive. This way.' She waved us into the building.

It was as grand inside as it was outside. I didn't have a chance to admire anything though, as Cleo shot off down the corridor at top speed. I had to jog to keep up with her. 'Would you like me to hold the bag?' I asked.

'No need.' **She held it tighter**. 'Do tell me about Rose,' she said. 'How did your grandma ... um ... acquire him?'

'She just ... um ... came across him,' I said. 'He's supposed to be lucky, actually.'

Cleo stopped dead. 'And is he?' she asked.

'Given we just **crashed into the sea**,' Piper said, 'I'm not so sure.'

Grandma tutted. 'We're all alive, aren't we? You don't get much luckier than that.'

Cleo raised her eyebrows. 'And have there been

111

any other ... um ... **fortunate** events?'

'We won some money, once,' Piper said.

'I got a place at dance school.' Thomas gave a twirl.

'Don't forget the amulet.' Grandma looked proud. 'Rose dug it up. I could hardly believe my eyes when I opened it and found the scroll. Apparently, it shows the location of a reputed potion of life.'

'So Geoffrey said.' Cleo smiled at us. 'I do love a puzzle. I shall do everything I can to help you.'

'How very kind,' said Grandma. 'Because we are in quite a hurry, actually. Ollie's hamster is on her last legs.'

'Gracious, how **terrible**.' Cleo dusted a speck from her collar.

'Having had the benefits of the potion explained by dear Geoffrey,' Grandma went on, 'we feel it could help.'

'You're not in it for the money then?' Cleo's eyebrows shot up again. 'How odd. Most treasure seekers are.'

'Well, cold hard cash would be nice,' Grandma admitted. 'I do have a balloon to fix. But my grandson's hamster is far more important.'

'Of course it is.' Cleo's teeth glinted. 'Let's get going then, shall we?'

18

Cleo strode down the corridor, pausing every now and then to make sure we were all still behind her, and to give Grandma's bag a little squeeze.

She finally stopped in front of a large set of doors.

'Here we are.' She gave a wave. 'The central chamber.'

She marched in.

We followed her.

Wow. I stared around.

The room was circular, and enormous – and **very glittery**. I could hardly see anything that wasn't gold. There wasn't a ceiling, just a huge glass dome high above us. Light flooded through on to a massive table which looked like it had been carved from a single slab of stone.

There was a velvet cushion in the centre of it.

It was a strange place for a cushion. I wondered why it was there.

Piper was admiring the statues. There were an awful lot of them. Standing all around the walls on marble plinths.

Statues of dogs.

Dogs that looked like Rose.

It was **CREEPY**.

Cleo saw me looking. 'Choodles were highly prized in ancient Egypt,' she said. 'They were the pets of the pharaoh.' She trotted over to the table and popped Grandma's bag on it. **'I can't wait to meet this one.** I've got him some biscuits and a special bed.' She plumped up the cushion.

'Rose is a Dog of Destiny.' Grandma sounded proud. 'Immortal, in fact. It says so on Wikipedia.'

Cleo gave a laugh. 'Only **Anubis**, the original Dog of Destiny, is immortal,' she said. 'And much as I would love your little doggy to be the real thing, the chances are he's just a descendant.'

'**A descendant?**' Grandma blinked.

Cleo nodded. 'Yes. Descendants don't have the reputed powers.'

'Is there a way to find out?' Piper asked. 'Some kind of test?'

Cleo giggled. 'There certainly is,' she said. 'But it takes a few days.'

I thought of poor Myrtle on her sickbed. 'We don't **have** a few days,' I said.

'There's no need for a test,' Grandma huffed. 'He's extremely lucky, and not only that, his name used to be Anubis. **I'm telling you. Rose is the real thing**.'

Cleo smiled. 'I do hope so.' She ripped open a box of bone-shaped biscuits and poured them into a dish. 'Wouldn't that be something? Anubis. The long-lost pet of King Tutti-Frutti, home at last.'

'He once belonged to a king?' Grandma looked thrilled.

'The **original** certainly did,' Cleo said. She put the empty box down and reached inside Grandma's bag. 'Welcome, little one,' she said.

She lifted Rose out.

Oh no.

We stared in horror.

Rose hung limply from her hands. His eyes were half closed.

He really was ill.

Grandma gasped and grabbed a biscuit. She wafted it under his nose.

Rose sighed and closed his eyes completely.

He didn't even lick it.

'It's serious.' Grandma went pale. 'You must call the vet immediately.'

'I'll fetch him now.' Cleo put Rose down on the cushion and trotted towards the door. 'Don't worry. He's local. We'll have Rose as right as rain in no time.'

Rose opened one eye and stared after her. When he saw me looking, he shut it again. I stared at him. **What was he up to?** For a minute there he'd looked absolutely fine. Cleo trotted back in. 'He's on his way. He'll be here any minute.'

'I hope he knows what he's doing.' Grandma clasped her hands. 'Rose is so precious.'

'He's the best,' Cleo reassured her. 'Cairo's **Vet of the Year**. A Choodle specialist, in fact.'

'Wonderful.' Grandma took a relieved bite of the biscuit she was still holding. 'Mmmm,' she said. 'Beefy.'

'Another?' Thomas offered her the bowl.

Piper frowned. 'How can the vet be a Choodle specialist?' she asked. 'When there are hardly any Choodles to practise on?'

Cleo blinked at her. She paused for a moment. 'He's a specialist in the legend,' she said. 'That's what I meant.'

'The legend?' Grandma leant forward. **What legend?'**

'Surely you've heard it?' Cleo seemed surprised.

Grandma shook her head. 'There wasn't anything on Wikipedia,' she said.

Cleo smirked. 'Then let me tell you,' she said.

'Anubis,' Cleo began, 'was the treasured pet of King Tutti-Frutti III. The pair were inseparable. In 1050 BC, the king decided to go on a hunting expedition. Foolishly, he didn't take his lucky little dog.'

'What a mistake,' Grandma tutted.

'It was.' Cleo nodded. 'The boat was rammed by an angry hippo. Tutti-Frutti died horribly.' She shuddered. '**They never found his head**.'

'**EW**,' Piper said.

Cleo went on. 'The uneaten bits of Tutti-Frutti were **mummified** and placed in a tomb, as was custom, along with his wives and several slaves.'

'How nice for them,' muttered Piper.

'But then' – Cleo's nostrils flared – 'something **even more terrible** happened.' She looked around dramatically.

I was interested to find out what could be more terrible than having your head eaten by a hippo.

We waited.

Cleo thumped her fist down on the stone table. **'Anubis.'**

'What about him?' Thomas said.

'Anubis had **disappeared**.' Cleo shook her head. 'People searched for days, but there was no sign of him. The king's uncle was suspected. He'd always envied his nephew's Choodle.'

'Shocking,' Grandma gasped. 'His own nephew's dog.'

'If Tutti-Frutti was dead,' Piper asked, 'why did it matter who had Anubis?'

'Because in those days,' Cleo said, 'pets were mummified along with their masters.'

Piper's mouth fell open. **'They mummified perfectly good pets?'**

'Oh yes.' Cleo nodded. 'To accompany them into **THE UNDERWORLD.'**

'That's awful.' Piper looked outraged.

Cleo took no notice of Piper's opinion. She carried on. 'As this meant the burial protocol was not followed, descendants of the king's uncle were struck down by a terrible **curse**.'

'**Oooh**. What was it?' Thomas clasped his hands in anticipation.

Cleo closed her eyes. She seemed to be struggling to speak.

We waited.

Her eyes snapped back open. 'Because of his uncle's treachery,' she hissed, '**every descendant of the king had a little toe that was longer than their big toe**.'

Eh? I'd been expecting a plague of locusts, or ... or ... rain for a thousand days or pox or something. 'It doesn't sound that appalling,' I said.

Cleo glared at me. 'Think how

hard it would be to find shoes, dear? Descendants of the king must have their shoes specially made. **The expense!** Not to mention small children pointing at your feet on the beach.'

'Surely toe length has more to do with **genes**,' Piper said, 'than whether a small dog was mummified or not?'

Cleo ignored her. She went on with the story. 'The curse extended to Anubis. **He must roam the earth until reunited with his master.**'

'So immortal until mummified?' Thomas said.

'That's right.' Cleo nodded. 'And he's been missing for three thousand years.'

'It's just a story,' Piper said. 'Dogs last longer than hamsters, but they still only live to about twelve.'

'It may be just a story.' Cleo scowled at her. 'But descendants of the king have always hoped that one day, Anubis would be returned to his master.'

'Why?' I asked.

Cleo rolled her eyes. 'Because then the curse would

be broken,' she said. '**All the overgrown toes would shrink back to the correct proportions.**'

Piper gave a snort. 'Surely they don't **REALLY** think that?' she said.

Cleo glared at her. 'They do. Why do you think Choodles are so rare?'

Grandma looked horrified. She clamped her hands over Rose's ears. 'They've been mummifying darling little dogs?' she mouthed. 'In the hope they're the real Anubis?'

'Not any more,' Cleo said, quickly. 'But in the past – yes. People were always claiming they'd found him.' She tutted. 'They hadn't, of course. Most were poodles. On the rare occasion a Choodle did turn up, a ceremony would take place.' She patted the stone table. 'On this, in fact. It's an **original mummification table**, so it seemed fitting.'

I moved away from it.

'A public holiday would be granted, and there would be a procession, with candyfloss and music

124

and the most wonderful dancing.' She gave a little demonstration.

Thomas applauded. 'You're very light on your feet,' he said.

Piper looked like she was going to explode. '**A party? For the mummification of a dog?**'

Cleo nodded. 'And all for nothing. The curse was never broken. None were the real Anubis.'

'That's horrible.' Piper looked like she was going to cry.

'That's what the high commissioner said, twenty years ago, when he banned the ceremonies.' Cleo tutted. 'Some felt it was a terrible blow to tradition.'

Grandma was looking nervous. 'So Rose is safe?'

Cleo held out her hands. 'Absolutely, Florence. While many would still like to get their hands on the **real** Anubis, the penalty for dog mummification is severe.'

'So it should be,' muttered Piper.

'You have nothing to worry about.' Cleo turned as

a door flew open behind her. 'Ah. Here's Amis.'

'**I came as quick as I could.**' A tall man wearing a surgical mask and a white coat burst in. '**Vere is the patient?**' He looked around.

'Just here.' Cleo waved towards the table. 'Such a treat, Amis. A darling Choodle.'

Amis shot over for a closer look. 'Vell, how very special.' He gave an excited giggle.

'He belongs to Florence, here.' Cleo gestured towards Grandma. 'He's her dear little pet. I have promised we will look after him very well indeed.'

'Of course.' Amis looked at Grandma, then smoothed back his very dark hair. 'I am delighted to meet you.' He held out his hand.

Grandma shook it. 'Can you help him?' she asked.

'I am sure.' Amis hovered over Rose. 'Let me see.'

He peered under an eyelid, and then took Rose's pulse.

Rose looked like he was trying to blend into the cushion.

'Interesting,' Amis muttered. He peered into Rose's ears.

Grandma looked on anxiously.

Amis stepped away from the table. He shook his head and sucked on his teeth. '**He is sick**.'

'How bad is it?' Grandma looked distraught.

Amis shook his head. 'I am afraid ee has ze doggy pox. Like chicken pox, but for dogs.'

'I can't see any spots,' Piper said.

'Zey will come.' Amis nodded.

'Can you **cure** him?' Grandma clutched her hands together.

'Of course.' Amis nodded reassuringly. 'A couple of days with me and he will be right as rain. I shall take him to the surgery and tend him there.'

'I'll come.' Grandma grabbed her bag.

127

'**No, no.**' Amis held up his hand. 'Ee must have peace and quiet. I have ze medicine. I vill return him to you just as soon as ee is better.'

He picked up the cushion with Rose still on it. 'No need to worry,' he called from the doorway. '**I am quality vet.**'

Grandma got a tissue out of her bag and blew her nose.

'Don't worry, Grandma.' I gave her a hug. 'I'm sure he'll be fine.'

'Of course he will,' said Piper.

Thomas did a pas de chat. 'I could see him perking up the second he was carried out,' he said.

'Really?' Grandma cheered up.

20

Cleo moved the biscuits off the table. 'We have a school visit later,' she said. 'I'll just get things ready for the demonstration, and then you can show me your treasure map.'

'What are you demonstrating?' Thomas asked.

'Mummification.' Cleo looked surprised. 'Of course.'

'**What?**' Piper shrieked. 'You **still** mummify stuff? For school visits?'

'Only things like tomatoes, dear. Sometimes a marrow. It's educational.'

'Oh.' Piper calmed down.

'Of course, on occasion,' Cleo said, 'someone brings along a much-loved pet, but they are always ... um ... past their best by the time they arrive on our table.' She paused. 'We get far too many hamsters, to be honest. One doesn't like to say no, but they're such fiddly little things.'

Hamsters? Fiddly?

I shuddered.

There was a bang from behind.

It was the door again.

This time a girl came in. She was wearing a white coat and pushing a trolley.

At first, I thought it might be a tea trolley, but I had a quick look, and it wasn't.

I could see a hacksaw and a drill – and lots of hooks.

There wasn't any cake.

'Mina!' Cleo rubbed her hands. 'There you are.' She introduced us. 'Mina does the gory stuff,' she said. 'I couldn't do it myself. I'm far too squeamish.'

'Hi.' Mina waved.

She didn't look that much older than us. She certainly wasn't as old as any of our teachers. Despite all the sharp stuff on the trolley, she looked quite friendly.

She tipped a box of syringes on to the table. 'Would you like to mummify something?' she said.

'**Oooh. Yes please**.' Thomas skipped over.

Piper and I took a step back. 'Mummify what, exactly?' I asked.

I wouldn't be able to do a hamster.

Mina held up a tomato.

'Oh. OK then.' I went over.

'I thought it took ages.' Piper joined me.

Mina shook her head. 'It used to, but we have new techniques. I can knock up a mummy in an afternoon, pretty much.'

'Amazing,' Grandma marvelled.

'One minute.' Mina ran to the wall by the door and pressed a button.

There was a creaking from above.

We looked up.

Something was coming down from the centre of the dome.

It looked like a scaffolding pole, with an enormous

131

toilet roll on it.

It came to a stop just above the table.

'It's bandage,' Mina explained. 'When we need it, we pull on the end.' She reached over and showed us. 'See?'

The roll spun, and she cut a length off. 'That should be enough.'

She passed a tomato to me, along with a crochet hook. 'Now,' she said, 'you make a tiny hole. Then you **disembowel** it.' She passed me a dish. 'For the innards.'

Woo! This was fun! I was just about to make a

start when Cleo interrupted. 'Mina. There's not time for this. Florence has business elsewhere, and the ... um ... schoolchildren will be arriving soon.' **She gave Mina a hard stare**.

'Sorry,' Mina said.

She took the tomato back.

21

Cleo was keen to get going. 'Where's the amulet?' she asked Grandma.

Grandma rummaged in her bag. 'Just here,' she said.

Cleo turned back to Mina. 'Have you everything you need?'

'Yep.' Mina arranged some **nasty-looking instruments** on the table. 'Don't rush back. The ... um ... schoolchildren will be here until teatime, at least.'

'Wonderful.' Cleo beamed at her. 'I shall see you afterwards.'

'You certainly will.' Mina sounded cheerful.

'This way.' Cleo clip-clopped into the corridor. She turned to Grandma. 'I'll look at the map as we're walking.'

Grandma snapped open the amulet and handed the tiny scroll to Cleo.

Cleo unrolled it. '**Aha**,' she said. 'I know exactly where this is.' She handed it back.

'You do?' Grandma looked surprised. 'You don't want to look in more detail?'

Cleo shook her head. 'It's a newly uncovered tomb. A sub-chamber of one of the great pyramids.' She smirked. 'It's very close. A mile from here, I'd say.'

'**Is that all?**' Grandma gave an excited clap. 'Hear that, Ollie? We'll have that potion made and back to Myrtle in no time.'

I hoped so.

'And the grid on the map.' Cleo clopped faster. 'The floor of the chamber is made of stone slabs, so—'

Grandma was almost running to keep up. 'We'll find the cross on one of those?'

'Exactly.'

Grandma looked thrilled. '**Wonderful**. This is all just falling into place.'

It was. It was nice of Cleo to help us. I was surprised she wasn't interested in keeping the potion for herself. Maybe ancient recipes were ten a penny in Egypt?

Things were going really well.

For now, anyway.

22

We went out the back way, as Cleo said there'd been some trouble out the front.

'Someone tried to climb over the gate,' she said. 'No need to worry. They've been apprehended by the guards.'

Piper looked confused. 'Why would anyone break in **here**?' she said.

Cleo shrugged. 'Maybe someone heard of your quest?' she said. '**That map is valuable**. Geoffrey is not always known for his discretion.'

'Honestly,' huffed Grandma. 'I **knew** he wouldn't be able to keep his mouth shut.'

'You mean **someone else** is after the potion?' I looked over my shoulder.

'Maybe.' Cleo bustled ahead. 'But don't worry. I'll accompany you there and make sure we're not

137

followed – though I'm afraid I won't be able to stay and help search. I have an ... um ... **prior** engagement.' She gave a small smile. 'Once you've found Baz's recipe, you can make your way back. Your little dog will be much improved by then, I'm sure.'

'I do hope so.' Grandma looked anxious.

'He's in the very best hands.' Cleo flagged down a passing tuk-tuk. 'In you get.'

Tuk-tuks are a cross between a motorbike and a golf buggy, and don't look very safe. I peered inside. **There weren't any seatbelts!** Mum wouldn't be very pleased about that. There wasn't much room either. I squashed myself into the back, next to Piper and Thomas. Grandma climbed into the front with Cleo. It seemed to be leaning a bit. **I hoped we weren't going to topple over**.

The driver revved and took off into the traffic. I shut my eyes and held on tight.

After a few minutes I opened my eyes to see if we were there yet.

We weren't. We'd **barely** moved. The driver kept shouting at other drivers and a couple of times he even got out to make his point.

Cleo checked her watch.

'Should we walk instead?' Piper said. 'You said it wasn't far.'

Walk?' Cleo's eyebrows shot up. 'Not in these shoes, dear.'

In the end she got the tuk-tuk to do a detour across a roundabout and along the pavements. I kept my eyes shut as that made me feel safer. By the time I opened them again we were in the desert. I checked behind to make sure we weren't being followed, but all I could see was dust.

Piper and Thomas were enjoying themselves. They shouted '**Yee-ha!**' every time the tuk-tuk flew up in the air. I concentrated on holding on. I wasn't enjoying the ride at all. It was horribly bumpy. I decided I must have left my explorer genes in Great Potton.

'Look!' Thomas jumped up. 'Over there.' He pointed. **'The pyramids! Aren't they incredible?'**

I squinted through the dust. There they were, ahead of us, rising from the sand. **Wow**. They looked just like the pictures we'd been shown at school. 'They're so **cool**,' I said.

Piper was more interested in the camels roaming about than the pyramids. 'Look at their funny faces,' she said. 'I might get one. I could keep it in the garden. Mum's always moaning about the grass.'

'You'd only have to feed it once a month,' Thomas said. 'They store food in their humps.'

Piper stared at him in delight. 'Mum can't argue with that, then,' she said. 'It'll practically look after itself.' She sat back, beaming. 'That's it. **If I'm ever allowed a pet, I'm having a camel**.'

23

As we got closer, Cleo pointed towards the largest pyramid. **'The final resting place of King Tutti-Frutti,'** she announced. 'The greatest pharaoh and Choodle owner of them all.'

'Choodle mummifier, you mean,' Piper said, crossly.

'It was ancient tradition,' Cleo said. 'You can't argue with tradition.'

Piper looked like she was going to, but she didn't get a chance. Cleo pointed again. 'See that small archway? Halfway up?'

We squinted in the sun.

'It's the entrance to a tunnel,' Cleo said. 'Leading directly to Tutti-Frutti's tomb. It was built so Anubis could be returned to his master. Who knew it would take so long to find him?' She gave a little laugh and patted Grandma's arm.

Piper blinked. 'All that fuss because a dog went missing?' she said. 'You'd have thought he'd have made do with something else, wouldn't you? Didn't he have a **hamster**?'

'**Hey**,' I objected.

'He was very fond of Anubis,' Cleo said. 'Just as you are of Rose.'

'That may be,' Grandma muttered. 'But when I am past my best, I will **not** insist my pets come with me.'

'**Ooh**. Can I have them?' asked Piper.

'Of course,' Grandma said generously.

Well, that was nice! **What about me?** I was her grandson. She hadn't considered that I might like a tarantula, or a naked mole rat or a ... oh, actually, Piper was welcome to them.

'I hope Rose is OK,' Piper said.

'I'm sure Angus is working his magic.' Cleo patted her arm. 'He's highly skilled.'

'**Angus?**' Piper looked confused. 'Who's Angus?'

143

'The vet.' Cleo looked surprised.

'I thought his name was **Amis**?' I said.

'No.' Cleo looked taken aback. 'His name's Angus. Angus the vet. I know him well.'

'It was **definitely** Amis,' Piper whispered.

'Maybe she isn't good with names?' I said. Mrs Jones at school is like that. Half the time she calls me Ronald because I remind her of someone she taught twenty-two years ago.

'You don't think she's up to something, do you?' Piper whispered.

I looked at her. 'Cleo? Like what?'

Piper shrugged. 'Maybe she wants Rose for herself?' she said. '**To sell?**'

I felt a bit uneasy. Cleo seemed OK. She was Head of Tourism, after all. I thought of her jewellery and shoes. 'She doesn't look like she needs the money.'

'What are you two whispering about?' Thomas whispered loudly.

'Just marvelling at the sand,' I said.

Cleo was still talking to Grandma about the tunnel. 'We've had to fit a steel door,' she said. 'Too many tourists were crawling in with selfie sticks. Taking pictures of themselves with the king. Disgraceful.'

Grandma tutted. 'You'd never catch me with a selfie stick,' she said. 'I mean, I **do** have one in my bag, but that's Piper's.'

Piper looked surprised. 'No it's not,' she said. '**It's yours**.'

Grandma ignored her. 'Do go on, Cleo,' she said.

'I alone have been entrusted with a key.' Cleo looked smug. 'I pop in occasionally. Make sure nothing's been nibbled by rats, do a spot of dusting. That sort of thing.'

'Isn't there a main entrance?' Piper asked.

Cleo nodded. 'Straight through the gift shop,' she said. 'But that one's locked too. Tourists can't be trusted. There are many other tunnels to the tomb, of course, but most were bricked up years ago.' Cleo tapped the driver on the shoulder. 'Stop here, please.'

We climbed out after her and trekked across the dunes. Cleo wasn't finding it easy in her heels. She kept sinking. Eventually she stopped. 'Here we are,' she said. 'They were digging foundations for an ice-cream parlour when they uncovered **this**.' She waved towards some stonework, half buried in the sand. 'It's the place on your map.'

I could see a dark cobwebby tunnel through the bars of a sunken gate. **I didn't like the look of it**. There'd be **dead things** down there. I didn't really feel like going in, but if I wanted to help Myrtle, I didn't have much choice.

'I'll just undo the chain.' Cleo tottered over and rotated the dials of a large padlock. 'In you go,' she said. 'Follow the passage to the end. Have you got your map?'

'It's here.' Grandma waved it. 'Are you sure you won't come with us?'

Cleo looked sorrowful. 'I adore a spot of treasure hunting,' she said. 'But I'm afraid I have some ... um

146

... business to be getting on with.'

We filed past her into the passage.

It was cold and damp.

Spooky.

There was a crash. I spun around.

Cleo had slammed the gate shut and pulled the chain back through! She snapped the padlock shut.

Eh?

She gave me a little wave. 'You don't want tourists disturbing you,' she said. 'Don't worry. I'll give you the combination.'

'OK,' I said. 'What is it?'

'One two, one two,' she said. 'As in one, two, buckle my shoe. Easy to remember.'

'**Wonderful**,' Grandma said. 'Many thanks for your help.'

'Any time.' Cleo turned and walked away. 'Don't step on any of the **mummies**.'

She vanished into the sunshine.

'**Come on, then.**' Grandma pulled on a head torch and took off down the passage.

'**Woo!** This is fun.' Piper and Thomas raced past me. 'Come on, Ollie.'

They seemed to be in quite a hurry to get to all the dead stuff.

I wasn't.

It felt like something **bad** was going to happen.

Maybe it was because Rose wasn't with us?

I hoped he was all right with Amis – or Angus – or whatever his name was. Grandma would be really upset if Rose became ... um ... past his best.

I took one last look at the blue sky outside and followed the others.

The only thing worse than walking through a spooky dark tunnel, is walking through a spooky dark tunnel **on your own**.

Something flew by my ear. OMG. Was that a bat?

Then something scurried across my foot.

I froze.

It could have been one of those **flesh-eating scarabs**. I'd seen them in films. Huge things, that burrow under your skin and ... and ...

I felt quite faint.

We were all going to die horribly, and Mum would neve—

Suddenly a light shone in my face.

'What are you doing, Ollie?'

Piper had come to find me.

I told her about the scarab and she shone her torch at the floor and pointed out that scarabs were quite small and had no interest in eating me.

I stared at her miserably. 'I **hate** it down here,' I said. 'I don't think I've got explorer genes after all.'

'Don't be silly,' Piper said. 'You just haven't

developed the "underground tunnel" ones yet. Give it time. Soon you won't even notice the insects and the spiders and the **dead** stuff.'

'Really?'

'Yes. Come—' She stopped suddenly. 'What's that **rattling** noise?'

'It sounds like the gate.' I looked at her in horror. 'Someone's trying to get in.'

'It's probably the wind,' Piper said. 'Stop worrying, Ollie. Come on. The sooner we find the recipe the better.'

I followed her down the passage. I still felt uneasy. Someone had tried to get into the town hall earlier, hadn't they? If you asked me, someone was after the map.

It didn't take long to catch up with the others. Grandma was shining her head torch around and marvelling about how we were the first people down here for **thousands** of years – but then Thomas spotted a half-eaten sandwich and a Mars bar wrapper, which reminded us that archaeologists had been here last week. I don't know why, but that made me feel a little bit better.

'**There**.' Grandma pointed ahead. 'The entrance to the chamber.'

'It's bricked up,' Thomas said.

Grandma shone her torch at it. 'There must be a way through.' she said. 'Tap it.'

'**Tap it?**' I looked at her.

'Yes. If we tap the right spot, I expect it will slide right back.'

'Um ... I think that only happens in films,' Piper said.

'It's worth a try.' Grandma sounded indignant.

'Or,' said Thomas, 'we could squeeze through that hole there, at the bottom?' He shone his torch towards the floor, where some bricks had been pulled out.

'Much simpler.' Grandma gave a little clap.

Thomas seemed keen to go first so I was happy to let him. Grandma went next and then I followed Piper.

Her bottom was blocking the light from Grandma's torch, so it was ever so dark. I concentrated on not panicking until the tunnel widened out a bit. Then I did panic because I thought I'd crawled through a **spider's web**, but it turned out to be Piper's hair, as she'd kindly stopped to wait for me.

By the time I reached the chamber on the other side, Grandma had taken off her head torch and popped it on a stone shelf. It cast a ghostly light over everything.

'What do you think, Ollie?' she said.

I looked around.

Scary, **cobwebby** and **freezing** were the first words that came to mind.

'Awesome,' I said.

'Isn't it?' said Piper.

The chamber was bigger than I expected and I couldn't see a sarcophagus, or any coffins, which was good. There were a lot of decorative pots. Most stood around the walls, but a few bigger ones were dotted about the floor. I was just admiring one when Thomas told me they were **canopic jars**.

I stared at him. 'What are canopic jars?' I said.

'They hold **leftover bits** from the mummies,' he explained. 'Livers, lungs, stomachs – though not the heart and kidneys. They leave those in.'

'Thanks, Thomas.' I stepped away from the jar. 'That's good to know.'

'Any time,' he said.

Grandma clapped her hands. 'Now,' she said. 'Stop chatting. We have a sick hamster depending on us, not to mention Rose. **Time is of the essence**. Let's start looking.' She waved the tiny map. 'There's a cross on one of these stone slabs,' she said. 'If we stand on it and look west, we should be able to see ...' She peered closely. 'A cat's face.'

'Then what?' Piper asked.

Grandma shrugged. 'Who knows. We'll either find Baz's recipe, or die horribly in an ancient Egyptian booby trap.'

Great.

'Have you heard from Mrs Frost again?' Piper asked, as we started to search. 'Is Myrtle any better?'

I shook my head. 'She's been asleep all day.'

'Isn't that **normal** for a hamster?' Piper asked.

'She usually wakes up for a mid-afternoon snack.' My voice **cracked** a little bit. 'Mrs Frost says she's not herself at all.'

'I hope she doesn't die before we get back with the potion,' Piper said. 'I really like Myrtle.'

'**So do I.**' I glared at her. 'So thanks for that thought.'

I stomped off into the least spidery-looking bit of the room and started to study the floor. The stone slabs were big and square, and I crouched down and looked really closely so I didn't miss anything.

I couldn't see a cross.

I backed slowly out into the centre of the room, looking all the while.

Going backwards probably wasn't the wisest idea, as I bumped into one of the canopic jars.

It tipped, though I managed to turn around and

grab it before it toppled completely. Phew. That could have made a nasty mess. I lowered the jar back into position. As I did, there was a click, and something trembled beneath my feet. **OMG! The slab I was standing on was moving!** I jumped off in horror and watched as it slid back into the wall, leaving a black hole in its place. **Blimey**. I could **have plummeted to my death!** Mum would certainly have had something to say about that.

The hole didn't look very inviting. I peered into it. **A ladder descended into darkness.**

I decided it must be one of the tunnels that led to

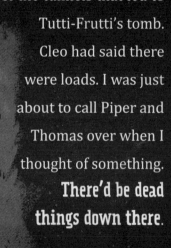

Tutti-Frutti's tomb. Cleo had said there were loads. I was just about to call Piper and Thomas over when I thought of something. **There'd be dead things down there**.

If I showed the others the hole, they'd probably want to explore.

It wasn't just about the dead stuff. We didn't have a lot of time. I had to think about Myrtle.

I gave the jar another push. **Bingo**. There was a click, and the slab slid back into place.

I sauntered over to Piper and Thomas. 'Hi,' I said. 'How are you getting on?'

'**I think we might have found it!**' Piper sounded excited. She shone her torch, so I could see. 'Just there. What do you think?'

I crouched down to have a look. She was right. **It was a cross**, a teeny one, faintly scraped into the stone. I reached out and touched it. **Wow**. Baz Basara had carved that, **four thousand years ago**. Incredible.

'It's here, Grandma,' I called.

'**Wonderful**.' Grandma gave a little clap and raced over to see. 'One step closer to everlasting hamsters. Look for the cat's face, everyone.'

Thomas spotted it first. 'There,' he said. He pointed

157

his torch at the jars lining the opposite wall. 'Painted on that urn. See?'

'**Well spotted**.' Grandma dashed over. 'Come on. I expect the recipe's stored inside it.'

I wasn't that keen on opening any of the jars, for reasons I might have mentioned before, so I let Piper and Thomas lift off the lid.

They stood on tiptoes and peered inside. 'It's empty,' Piper said. *Totally*. There's not even any body parts.'

'Are you sure?' Grandma pushed them out of the way and had a look herself. 'Maybe someone got here **before** us?'

'How could they?' Piper said. 'I thought we had the only map.'

'Maybe that wasn't the right cat?' Thomas swung his torch around, but we couldn't see another one.

I sat down. **This was awful**. If we couldn't find the recipe, what would become of Myrtle?

Then I saw something. Low on the wall, behind the cat urn.

Carvings.

I jumped to my feet. '**Look!**'

Grandma gasped. '**Hieroglyphs. A whole list!**' She gave me a hug. '**We've found it! Baz Basara's potion of life!**'

'**Woo!**' Thomas helped me move the urn out of the way.

Piper peered closely. 'I wonder what they mean.'

'Don't worry,' Grandma said. 'I'll copy them, and we'll work it out.' She rummaged in her bag for a pen.

I took a look myself. The top carving was definitely a hippo, and there was an arrow pointing to his mouth.

'**Hippo's tooth**.' Grandma pulled a notepad from her pocket and flipped it open. 'A very popular ingredient in ancient Egypt.' She wrote it down.

'That's a **nettle**.' Piper pointed to a scribble of a plant.

'What's that?' Thomas tilted his head.

'It's the Nile,' Grandma said. '**Nile mud**, I expect.'

There were about eight other drawings, which included a scorpion's sting, a porcupine quill and honey.

Grandma wrote them all down, and Piper took a picture on her phone for backup.

Baz Basara's Potion of Life.

We'd found it.

Thank goodness for that.

25

As we headed back down the tunnel, Grandma looked thoughtful. She waved her notepad. 'I might,' she said, 'tell Cleo we searched in vain.'

'Why?' Piper asked

Grandma sniffed. 'If she knows we found the recipe, she'll **insist** on seeing it.'

'So?' I said.

Grandma looked sulky. 'Once we've used the potion on Myrtle, I'm going to do the miracle cream thing. You know. In the pots. **I don't want her stealing my idea**.'

'Do you think she would?' Piper asked.

'Probably,' Grandma said. 'She looks the type.'

We got to the gate and it was brilliant to be back in the daylight. I hadn't liked it underground much. I had a quick look through the bars to make sure no one was lying in wait to steal our map, then reached for the padlock.

'One two, one two.' Piper reminded me of the combination.

'**I know**,' I said.

I spun the dials and pressed the button, but it didn't snap open. **Eh?** I tried again. One two, buckle my shoe, she'd said, hadn't she?

It **still** didn't work.

Then Piper had a go, and so did Thomas.

'Maybe it was three four, knock at the door?' I said.

'Five six, pick up sticks?' Piper suggested.

'Don't worry,' Grandma said. 'I've got a hairgrip.'

She took one out of her bag and started to pick the lock. That didn't work, so she picked up a boulder and **walloped** it instead.

'All done.'

'I think you've broken it,' I said.

'Of course I haven't.' Grandma chucked the bits of lock to one side.

We were out. After the cool of the passage, it was boiling. I looked across at the pyramids. 'Can we get a drink from the gift shop?' I asked.

'Ooh, yes.' Thomas flapped his arms around. 'Or an ice-cream. **I'm melting**.'

'Good idea,' Grandma said. 'I'll see if they've got a hippo's tooth.'

We trudged across the sand. It took ages as Piper kept on going over to camels to assess their suitability as pets.

'They're quite big up close,' she said. 'And not very friendly. I'll need to choose something more approachable if Mum's going to agree.'

The gift shop didn't sell water or hippo's teeth, so we went to the café next door. I didn't want to waste time, but Grandma said if we were going to do this properly, we needed a meeting.

The café was busy, but we found a table with a view of the pyramids and sat down.

Grandma flipped open her pad. 'First things first,' she announced. 'We need to source all of these ingredients. Piper?'

'Yes?'

'You can find some **scorpion stings**. Two or three should do it. Thomas?'

'Yes?'

'You're in charge of **hippo teeth**. Ollie? You can track down a **porcupine**.' She picked up the menu and looked at it. 'I might have a cake.'

I blinked. 'So what are you going to ... um ... source?'

'I'll get the **Nile mud** before we leave,' Grandma said. 'I can pick up the honey from Tesco when we're back.'

'The **difficult** stuff, then?' I said.

'I'll get the nettles as well,' Grandma huffed. 'And

I need to get back to the town hall to check on Rose, remember.'

Piper looked up at the archway Cleo had pointed out earlier. 'I still can't believe they built a whole tunnel for a missing dog,' she said.

'Well, Rose was very important in his day.' Grandma looked proud.

I looked at her. 'Do you really believe he's the **original Dog of Destiny?**' I said.

Grandma blinked. 'Of course he is,' she said. 'I don't need Cleo's tests to tell me he's special.'

'I didn't say he **wasn't** special,' I said. 'It's just that three thousand is old for a dog.'

'To be fair, Ollie,' Piper said, 'Myrtle's six, and that's old for a hamster.'

'I know,' I said. 'But that's because I look after her so well. **She's not immortal**.'

'She might be soon.' Grandma tapped her notepad. 'Once we've made this.'

I don't really believe in magical stuff, and I was

pretty sure the potion wasn't going to make anything live for ever, but if it could help Myrtle get better, then that would be **brilliant**. I checked my phone. Mrs Frost had sent another text. It was better news. 'Myrtle's had half a carroty treat,' I told the others. 'She's brighter.'

'That's a relief,' Piper said. 'It'll take us **ages** to make the potion, and even then, it might not work.'

'No need to be positive,' I said.

Grandma was still looking over at the pyramid. The waitress who came to take our order must have noticed. She bent down towards us.

'Are you here for the **return**?' she whispered.

'**The return?**' I looked up from the menu. 'What do you mean?'

The woman rearranged our cutlery. 'I have a great friend at the town hall. She said we would have extra customers today.'

'I'm not surprised. The basbousa looks delicious,' Grandma said. 'I'll have that, with extra syrup.'

The waitress wrote it down. 'Are you descendants?' she asked.

'Descendants of who?' I asked.

The waitress smiled. 'Of the great pharaoh, of course.'

I was about to say no, but Thomas got in first. '**We are**,' he said. '**Direct** descendants, in fact. We were told to come, but not why.' He looked at her expectantly.

The waitress checked over her shoulder. Then she stooped back down.

'I bring good news,' she muttered. 'The little dog, Anubis. **It is back**. This time they are sure it is the real thing.'

Grandma froze.

'Anubis?' I said, as politely as I could.

The woman nodded enthusiastically. '**It is being mummified as we speak**, and this afternoon it will be returned to the tomb in a secret ceremony.' She got out her pad. 'Now. Who else would like the cake?'

We charged across the sand.

'Over there. That tuk-tuk.' Thomas pointed.

'I **knew** she was up to something.' Grandma looked furious. 'Wait till I see her.'

'I hope we're not too late.' Piper was pale despite the heat.

'Of course we won't be.' Grandma threw herself into the tuk-tuk.

I followed her. 'That's why Rose didn't want to come to Cairo,' I said. '**He knew they'd still be looking for him.**'

'Where's the driver?' Piper looked around.

'I'll do it.' Thomas hopped into the front. 'Ready?'

Hey! I'd have driven if I'd known it was an option.

'**Go**,' Grandma shouted. 'Put your foot down.'

We revved away in a cloud of dust.

'Oh. There he is.' Piper pointed.

'Who?' I hung on for dear life.

'The driver. He doesn't look very pleased.'

I had a look. **He really didn't**.

'He got in another one,' Piper said. 'He's after us.' She paused. 'Oh dear.'

'What?'

'It's not **just** him,' she said.

I glanced behind. Piper was right. It wasn't just the driver. He must have had some friends.

There was a whole fleet of tuk-tuks chasing us.

'Faster, Thomas,' Grandma yelled.

Thomas obliged.

Then we went over a **bump**.

I'm not sure how Piper and Thomas managed to stay in.

I didn't.

Nor did Grandma.

We landed in a dune.

The fleet of tuk-tuks shot past us in a monster

169

cloud of dust. '**Quick**.' Grandma pulled me to my feet. 'This way.'

All I could see was billowing sand.

'I'll give you a leg up.' She shoved me on to something large and shaggy. **Eh?** **What was it?** A sofa? There was a lurch and I rose up. **OMG. I was on a camel.**

Grandma appeared beside me. Her camel was even bigger than mine.

She was brandishing her selfie stick.

'**This is hardly the time**, **Grandma**,' I shouted. '**We need to rescue Rose**.'

Oh. She wasn't taking a photo.

She reached over and gave my camel a prod. **Giddy-up**,' she shouted.

Blimey.

I had no idea camels could run so fast.

I held on for dear life.

OMG IT WAS SO BUMPY.

I was **never** getting on a camel again. Every bit of me was rattling. It didn't help that my pants were full

of sand. There was a lot of chafing.

'OK, Ollie?' Grandma called over.

'Oh yes,' I called back. **'Great fun.'**

171

We caught up with Thomas and Piper at a roundabout in the centre of Cairo. Everyone seemed to have been confused by Thomas's driving, which was good. There was such a **blur** of tuk-tuks going around in different directions, no one noticed them nipping off down a side street.

Grandma and I cantered behind.

'There's the Town Hall.' She pointed ahead. 'They've shut the gates. **Just wait until I see Cleo.**'

Thomas had screeched to a halt on the pavement. Piper blinked when she saw me on a camel. 'Didn't you like Thomas's driving?' she said.

'No,' I said. I slid down. It wasn't a very graceful dismount, **but a dog's life was at stake**. I looked up at the gates. They were ever so high. 'Shall we climb over?' I said. 'Or try round the back?'

'Neither,' Piper said. *Look. They're opening!*

'Someone's driving out.' Thomas jumped out of the way of a black limousine. The windows were tinted, but we could still see in.

There, in the back, was a small stone sarcophagus.

A dog-shaped sarcophagus.

I looked at Grandma in horror.

We were too late.

'**He wasn't in** it.' Grandma charged past the guards and up the steps.

Eh? I ran after her. 'How do you know?

Grandma waved her phone. 'He swallowed the tracker, remember? I can see him on this. **He's still in the town hall**.'

'Alive?' Piper caught up with us.

'The tracker's moving,' Grandma said. 'So he must be.'

'**Yay**.' Thomas gave a leap of joy.

We tore along the corridor and into the central chamber.

Mina was there, wiping the table.

'**Where's Rose?**' Grandma ran over.

'Shhh.' Mina looked around. 'Cleo hasn't left yet. She's deciding what to wear for the ceremony.'

'Is he here?'

'He **might** have escaped.' Mina gave us a wink. 'He was **very** wiggly.'

'So he's safe?'

'Yes.'

Piper gave her a hug. 'Thank you, Mina.'

'That's OK,' she said. 'Cleo got an **excellent** mummy. My best yet. I was really proud of it.'

'What was in it?' I asked.

'A marrow, four courgettes and an orange.'

'Where is he?' Grandma asked again.

Mina went over to an alcove at the back of the room. She pulled back a curtain.

Rose! There he was. Snoozing on a cushion. With ... was that another Choodle?

'Oh MY.' Piper ran over. **'Rose has got a friend.'**

'Ela's mine,' Mina said.
'I gave her a perm.
Cleo thinks she's a
cockapoo.'

'**She's adorable**.' Piper ruffled her fur. 'You're so lucky.'

'You'd better hide Rose.' Mina looked anxious. 'Cleo will be back soon.'

'Righto.' Grandma picked Rose up and popped him in her handbag.

Just in time.

Cleo clopped into the room. She looked mighty fine. She was wearing a **gold cloak** and an **enormous headdress**. She'd changed her shoes for some that were even higher and covered in crystals.

She stopped dead when she saw us.

'**Gracious**.' She blinked. 'Back already?'

'That's right. We are,' Grandma said.

'Did you find the recipe?' Cleo asked.

'No,' Grandma lied. 'We didn't.'

'Never mind,' Cleo said. 'At least you tried.' She gave a twirl. 'What do you think? I've got an event this afternoon.'

'Love the heels,' Thomas said, politely.

'Thank you.' Cleo looked pleased. 'I won't mention how much they cost.'

'We'd have been back sooner, but the lock on the gate jammed.' Grandma gave her a pointed look.

'Tut,' Cleo said. 'It's **always** doing that.'

'How's Rose?' Grandma asked. 'I was terribly worried about him. We came straight back to see how he was.'

Cleo brushed some fluff from her cloak. 'I'm afraid I have sad news about your doggy.'

'You do?' Grandma's eyebrows shot up.

'**He didn't make it**.' Cleo inspected a nail.

Grandma clutched the edge of the table. '**He didn't?**'

Cleo shook her head. 'Andrew did—'

'**Amis**,' Mina corrected her.

'That's right. **Amis** tried everything – he really is a wonderful vet – but your darling pet passed away ...' She checked her watch. 'About an hour ago.'

Grandma clutched herself dramatically while the rest of us looked as sad as we could. Thomas did a

177

particularly good job of throwing himself about and wailing.

Cleo patted her hair. 'I must go.' She adjusted her cloak. 'It's been lovely meeting you all. Sorry about your dog.'

She swept out the door. 'Toodle pip.'

We almost got away with it.

We would have done if Thomas hadn't done an unexpected arabesque and knocked the clockwork gerbil out of Piper's pocket.

She made a grab for it, but it landed on the floor.

The jolt must have switched it on because it shot across the room and down the corridor after Cleo.

Rose forgot himself.

There was no stopping him. He leapt out of Grandma's bag and tore after it, yipping.

No!

We sprinted after him.

I hadn't meant to knock Cleo over, but her heels were very high, and Rose had unbalanced her first by running through her legs.

'Sorry.' I charged past her.

'Don't apologise to her, Ollie,' Piper said.

'Sorry,' I said. I looked over my shoulder. Cleo was staring after Rose in astonishment.

'Quick,' I said.

'She'll never catch us in those heels,' Grandma said.

Thomas stopped. 'I'll keep her at bay.' He did a **threatening pirouette**. 'This was my fault. You catch Rose.'

He started doing the can-can.

Blimey. I wouldn't want to face Thomas's flying feet. There was no way Cleo would get past those.

Luckily, the gerbil had run out of steam. Rose savaged it, and that gave Grandma the chance to grab him.

'Come on.' She raced outside.

Thomas aimed a final high kick at Cleo and ran after us.

We hurled ourselves down the steps. Thank goodness. The gates were still open. **'GET BACK HERE.'** Cleo was purple as she teetered after us. **'THAT DOG BELONGS TO THE KING.'** **'Not any more,'** Grandma said. We charged out on to the street.

It was really busy. We'd definitely be able to shake her off.

'Which way?' Piper asked.

'Right,' Grandma said.

We turned right.

Oh no. It was a dead end. 'Left,' I said.

We ran. And then we ran some more. We dashed down tiny streets and up alleys and into a market on the quay.

There were loads of people milling round. Surely we'd lost Cleo by now?

I glanced over my shoulder.

We hadn't. Her headdress was bobbing behind us in the crowd.

I saw a gap between two stalls. 'This way,' I shouted to the others.

They followed me.

Oops.

'Bum,' I said.

'Well, that was clever,' Piper said.

We'd run out on to a jetty.

'Is this the Nile?' I stared at the river flowing in front of us.

'It certainly is.' Grandma nodded.

'It looks deep,' Thomas said. 'Is that a **hippo?'**

'There's loads of crocs.' Piper edged backwards.

Even if there hadn't been so much wildlife, the opposite bank was a long way away. A lot more than fifty metres. I turned. Was there any chance Cleo hadn't followed us?

No.

There she stood, **glowering** at us. She'd lost one of her shoes and was brandishing the other. **'Bring that dog back,'** she shouted. **'You can't escape.'**

Piper gasped. 'Look at her little toes,' she said. 'They're really **long**. She must be one of Tutti-Frutti's descendants!'

Things suddenly made sense. 'That's why she's desperate to break the curse,' I said. **'She thinks her toes will shrink back.'**

'It must be hard to buy nice shoes with unusual feet.' Thomas sounded sympathetic.

'That's no reason to mummify pets.' Piper glared at him.

'She looks very cross,' Grandma said. 'Has anyone got a plan?'

'Can you do the can-can thing again, Thomas?' Piper asked.

'I can try,' Thomas said. 'But I really need a big skirt to do it properly.'

Cleo stepped menacingly on to the jetty. Maybe we should swim for it? I glanced down at the water. It didn't look very nice, green and smelly an—

'Ollie.' Piper grabbed my arm. **'Look.'**

Thomas saw what she was pointing at and took a step back.

So did I. A small white motor cruiser was powering towards the jetty. It was going ever so fast. Too fast to stop, it looked like. OMG. It was going to ram us, wasn't it? We'd be flung into the Nile like ninepins. A dark figure stood at the wheel. It must be the person who wanted the map. They could have just asked. We'd finished with it, after all.

This wasn't going to end well. I closed my eyes.

'Someone's waving,' I heard Thomas say.

I opened my eyes again.

Blimey. The person on the deck was Mina.

She swung the cruiser alongside the jetty. 'Jump,' she shouted.

•••

'Thanks' I said, once we'd all scrambled aboard.

'No problem.' Mina skilfully avoided a hippo.

'Is this your boat?' Thomas said.

'Not really,' Mina said. 'I borrowed it.'

'Wonderful.' Grandma beamed. 'People are so generous with their things, aren't they?'

'They certainly are,' Mina said.

Grandma draped Rose around her neck. 'I haven't had a chance to thank you.'

'That's OK,' Mina said. 'Cleo's always bringing in Choodles. I wait till she's gone and let them straight out the back.'

'She really believes she can break the curse?' Piper said.

Mina giggled. 'She wants prettier feet.'

Piper rolled her eyes. 'Feet are feet. No one's are nice.'

'I beg to differ.' Thomas looked cross. 'Mine are exquisite.'

'Ollie?' Piper said.

'What?'

She pointed behind the boat. 'Someone's following us.'

I could see a column of spray in the distance. 'Is that a jet-ski?'

Thomas looked worried. 'Do you think it's Cleo?'

Grandma pulled out her spyglass and peered through it. 'Hard to tell. I don't think so.'

'Maybe it's the person Mina "borrowed" the boat from?' I suggested.

'Or someone after the recipe.' Grandma patted her bag.

Mina moved the throttle up a notch. 'Don't worry,' she said. 'Whoever it is, we're definitely faster.'

I hoped we were. Maybe we should park up and escape on foot? I glanced over at the river bank.

Oh dear.

Piper saw my face. 'What's wrong?' she asked.

I pointed at a moving cloud of dust. 'Cleo and Amis. They're chasing us on camels.'

'Horrible thieving dog thieves,' Grandma muttered. 'If they think they're going to get their mummifying hands on Rose, they can think again.'

Rose yapped in agreement.

Piper peered through the spyglass. 'They look ever so cross,' she said.

'They're miles away,' Thomas said. 'They'll never catch us.'

'Even so,' Mina said, 'I'll head for the other bank.' She spun the wheel.

There was a crunch.

'Oops.' Mina looked over the side. 'We hit a rock.'

'Hole in the hull,' Thomas shouted. 'We're taking on water.'

I glanced behind. The jet-ski was approaching fast. I looked down at the crocodiles. There were an awful lot of them, lying there, basking in the sun. 'Do you think we'll sink?' I asked.

'Probably.' Mina looked worried.

'Nobody panic,' Grandma said. She unwound Rose

from her neck and popped him back in her bag. 'I've got a plan.'

'Oh goody.' Piper clapped her hands. 'What is it?'

'We'll use the crocs as stepping stones,' Grandma said. She climbed up on to the rail.

I stared at her in horror. 'Are you joking?' I said.

'No.' She started to lower herself down. 'Come on.'

'I'm not doing that,' I said. 'It's too dangerous.'

Thomas climbed after Grandma. 'If the boat sinks, we'll end up in the water anyway,' he said.

'Have you got a better idea?' Piper looked at me.

'No,' I said.

'Well then,' she said. 'This'll give you a chance to develop your "walking on reptiles" gene, won't it?'

29

Grandma had lowered herself on to the scaly back of the closest crocodile. 'They're fast asleep,' she called. 'It's fine.'

She stood there for a moment, then took a giant stride on to the back of the next. And the next. And the next. They didn't stir. With one final leap she was on the shore.

'**My turn**.' Thomas bounded lightly after Grandma.

'Come on, Ollie.' Piper followed him.

I climbed up on the rail.

I could hear Mum's voice in my head. '**Don't you dare, Ollie**,' it screeched.

I hesitated.

'Are you going, Ollie?' Mina climbed past me. 'Or shall I?'

'After you,' I said, politely.

'**Hurry**,' Grandma shouted, as Mina landed beside her. '**A couple of them are stirring**.'

Oh. Great. They **would** wait till my turn, wouldn't they?

I scrambled over the side.

Whoa. Crocs are slippy.

I got my balance and jumped on to another one. I stood there, teetering.

'Ollie,' Piper bellowed. 'For goodness sake. Get a move on.'

I was about to do what she said when the one in

front of me twitched his tail.

I gulped. **Now what?**

Should I keep going? Or go back?

I turned to check my options.

It turned out I didn't have any. The croc behind had swum off.

I'd have to carry on heading for shore.

Then the one I was standing on moved.

I wobbled.

I wobbled and then I fell off.

Into the dark swirling waters of the Nile.

I was going to be eaten.

Mum would be furious.

OMG. The croc. The croc had me. I kicked frantically.

The croc hoisted me up and out of the river.

OH. It wasn't a croc.

I was face to face with Beatrix.

BEATRIX???

•••

Beatrix parked up the jet-ski while I spat out bits of Nile.

'I hope you've got some of that hand sanitiser left.' She sounded cross. 'This water's **filthy**.'

'Are you OK, Ollie?' Piper rushed over.

I nodded.

Beatrix glared at Grandma. 'You're very irresponsible,' she said. 'Wait till Sukey hears about this.'

'He's got his fifty-metre badge.' Grandma glared back. 'He was fine. How did you find us?'

Beatrix pointed at me. 'He's got an app on his phone. I tracked him.'

Oh. I'd forgotten about that.

Piper gasped. 'Were you the person who climbed over the town hall gates?'

Beatrix looked defiant. 'Maybe,' she said.

'**Blimey**.' Thomas looked at her with admiration. 'They were ever so high.'

'Did you try and follow us underground?' Piper

asked. 'Someone rattled the gate.'

Beatrix nodded. 'It was locked, so I popped into the gift shop to wait. I admit, I did rather allow myself to be distracted by the choice of tea towels. The next time I checked my phone you were heading for the Nile.'

'But how did you get to Egypt in the first place?' I asked.

Beatrix blushed. She looked down at her feet. 'I flew,' she said.

'**OMG**.' I stared at her in shock. 'That was Dad's plane. **You stole it.**'

'I **borrowed** it,' Beatrix said.

'I didn't even know you could fly.' I was dumbfounded.

'There was an instruction booklet,' Beatrix said. 'It wasn't hard to follow.'

Grandma looked outraged. '**I can't believe you stole George's plane**,' she said.

Beatrix scowled. 'It was **my** turn to have Ollie. I'm

fed up with you being the favourite grandma.'

'Even so,' Grandma tutted. **'You should never steal**. It's a terrible example to these fine young people.' She put her hand on my shoulder. 'What will Ollie's dad say when he finds out?'

Beatrix hung her head. 'I was hoping you wouldn't tell him,' she muttered.

Grandma looked thoughtful. 'I **suppose** if we don't mention Egypt at all ... ?'

'Egypt?' Beatrix flicked a river snail off her jacket. 'I don't know what you're talking about. **I've never been to Egypt.**'

'Nor have I,' Grandma said. 'Who'd want to? I've heard it's **very dull.**'

'Excuse me,' Mina said. 'But shouldn't we get going?'

I looked up. Cleo and Amis were cantering towards us at a furious pace. There was no way we could get away.

We'd have to take them on.

'I'm ready!' Grandma whipped out her selfie stick.

'As am I.' Beatrix stepped behind Grandma.

The camels screeched to a halt. Cleo wasn't looking quite so fine now. Her cloak was covered in dust and the headdress had dents all over it. Amis's white coat was no longer white. Nor was his surgical mask, which for some reason, he was still wearing.

'Get them, Albert,' Cleo shouted. **'Remember what's in it for you.'**

'Amis,' Amis hissed at her. 'We agreed **Amis**. And I did my bit.'

'Even so, Arthur, I am the one with the money.' Cleo smiled sweetly at him. 'Now hop off your camel and get that dog.'

195

'**We said Amis**.' He jumped down. 'Hand it over,' he said.

Grandma gave him a jab with her selfie stick. '**Absolutely not**.'

'Anubis belongs to the pharaoh.' Cleo trotted her camel around us. 'You must let me have him. **I need to break that curse**.'

'It won't make any difference,' I said to her. 'Your feet will stay the same.'

'You don't know that.' Cleo glared at me. 'We've never returned the real dog before.'

Mina put her hand up. 'Just to set the record straight,' she said. 'You've mainly returned courgettes. Though once we'd run out, so I used a butternut squash.'

Cleo gave her a furious look. 'When I have returned Anubis, I shall be giving your job to someone who has greater respect for the traditions of Egypt,' she said.

'I was leaving anyway.' Mina stuck her tongue out.

'Can we have less of the chat?' Amis sounded

annoyed. '**Just hand the dog over**. I went to a lot of trouble to get it here. I'm not giving up now.'

'What do you mean, a lot of trouble?' I stared at him.

Amis sniggered. He unhooked his surgical mask and let it dangle from his ear.

Blimey, what a massive moustache. If it was grey, instead of black, he'd look lik—

'Geoffrey?'

Grandma shrieked.

30

My mouth dropped open. Geoffrey? **OMG. It was Geoffrey**. What was he doing here?

'I thought you were an archaeologist?' Piper looked confused.

'That's right.' He twirled his moustache and gave a little bow. 'I am.'

'You offered to help.' Grandma blinked. 'You translated my map.'

'I did.' Geoffrey smirked. 'The one your dog so conveniently dug up for you.'

I stared at him. '**Did you bury the amulet?**' I asked.

Geoffrey preened. 'I certainly did. With a sausage. Choodles love sausages.'

'I knew it smelt meaty,' Piper said.

'**SO THE MAP WASN'T REAL?**' Grandma looked horrified. '**YOU DREW IT YOURSELF?**'

'I **TOLD** you that was felt tip,' Piper said to Thomas.
Geoffrey smirked. 'You all fell for it.'

'I didn't,' Piper said.

Oh no. **Myrtle**. I looked at Geoffrey in horror. 'So
the potion of life? It's not real? You made it up?'

'No. It's a real recipe. It's from my archives.'
Geoffrey preened. 'It had to sound authentic or you
might have got suspicious.'

Grandma stepped forward. 'So it could work then?
On hamsters, at least?'

'No idea.' Geoffrey shrugged. 'No one's made it for
years. I mean, **why would they?** No one believes that
sort of rubbish any more.'

'Cleo seems to,' Piper said, 'or she wouldn't be
trying to mummify Rose. Why are you helping her?'

Geoffrey smirked. 'Archaeology is expensive. I'd
run out of funds for my dig. That's why I was in Great
Potton. Visiting my aunt.'

'So that bit was true?' Grandma sniffed.

'Yes. I thought she might give me some cash, but

the old bat said I'd had enough already.' Geoffrey scowled at the memory. 'She had the paper open on the table. I was about to storm out when I saw your picture. You were holding a Choodle! **A Choodle!** I could hardly believe my eyes. I was so excited, I did a little dance.'

'A dance? Did you?' Thomas asked. 'I'd love to see it.'

I stepped on his foot.

'I knew Cleo had been trying to find the real Anubis for years,' Geoffrey went on. 'I gave her a call. Said I was sure I'd found him. **She was thrilled**. She said if I brought him to Cairo, she'd fund the rest of my dig.' He gave a snigger. 'I was going to steal him, but decided it'd be easier if you brought him yourselves. I was pretty sure a magic potion would do it.'

'**MY** suggestion,' Cleo called from her camel.

Geoffrey scowled at her. '**<u>IT WAS DEFINITELY MY IDEA</u>**,' he said. He turned back to Grandma. 'I'd brought the amulet as a gift for my aunt. It was a cheap one, from a souvenir stall. I pinched it back, popped in the map and buried it outside your tent.'

'Then once Rose had dug it up, you followed me to the library,' Grandma said.

'That's right.' Geoffrey beamed. 'Before heading back to Cairo and preparing for your arrival.'

'You dyed your hair,' Thomas said.

Geoffrey patted it proudly. 'I rather like it.'

'It looks **ridiculous**,' Grandma huffed. 'You're too <u>OLD</u> for that colour.'

'Was it you who carved the hieroglyphics on to the wall?' Piper asked him.

'Yes.' Geoffrey preened again. 'Rather good, weren't they? It was Cleo's job to take you there and lock you in. Keep you out of the way. We weren't going to let you out until after the ceremony.' He gave Cleo a sour look.

'**That was your fault**,' Cleo shouted down from her camel. 'You used a cheap padlock.'

'Where's the dog?' Geoffrey looked menacing.

'No idea,' Grandma said.

Rose stuck his head out of her bag. He yipped defiantly.

Geoffrey glared at Grandma. **'Hand him over,'** he said. **'I need the money.'**

'NO.' Grandma kept him at bay with her selfie stick. She passed her bag to Piper.

Piper passed it to me.

Geoffrey turned and headed in my direction.

I looked behind, but there was no one for me to pass the bag to.

Thomas started doing high kicks, but Geoffrey didn't stop. Piper jumped in front of him, but he pushed her aside.

He was coming straight for me.

I clutched the bag tightly as he approached. Maybe I could kick him in the shins?

I didn't need to.

WHACK. The cabbage came from nowhere, knocking Geoffrey's feet from under him. He

somersaulted into the air and landed face first in the mud.

Grandma spun around. '**Beatrix?**'

Beatrix hefted another cabbage. She looked very pleased with herself. 'I'm not captain of the Bowls Club for nothing,' she said.

Geoffrey seemed pretty cross about being bowled over with a cruciferous vegetable, but between us we managed to wrap him in an old bit of fishing net. Grandma sat on him and gave me her phone to call the high commissioner.

'No need,' Mina said. 'I've already called him. He's on his way.'

Cleo must have realised the game was up. **She'd galloped off into the distance**.

'**Good riddance**,' Grandma shouted after her. '**Don't come back, you dog thief, you**.' She turned to Beatrix. 'Well done with the cabbages,' she said. 'Where did you find them?'

'The river,' Beatrix said. 'I had to wrestle one away from a hippo.'

'**Gracious**.' Grandma looked impressed.

'Now.' Beatrix brushed herself down. 'We need to get home. I don't want those craft materials going to waste ... Ollie? Are you all right?'

I wasn't listening.

I'd noticed something.

Something awful.

'Grandma,' I said. '**Where's your bag?**'

31

'**Ha,**' **Geoffrey said,** from his net. 'Cleo took it. She's got your dog. HahahahahaOW.'

'Sorry.' Beatrix stepped off his hand.

Grandma stared after the dust cloud.

Beatrix put an arm around her. 'There, there,' she said.

I felt awful. I'd had the bag last. I'd put it down to help with Geoffrey.

Now Cleo had it.

CLEO HAD ROSE.

•••

Last time I was on a camel, I'd sworn never to go on one again, but this was an emergency. **It was my fault Rose had gone. I was going to get her back.** No one was watching, so I scrambled on to Geoffrey's camel and sat between its humps. '**Giddy-up,**' I said.

It started munching one of the cabbages.

'Hey.' Piper looked up. 'What are you doing?'

'Going after Cleo,' I said. 'If I can get the camel to start.'

'Hang on.' Piper scrambled up behind me.

'I'm coming.' Thomas clambered on to one of the humps.

We sat there. 'What now?' I said.

'Giddy-up.' Thomas gave a bounce.

The camel took more notice of Thomas than it had of me. **It cantered off at top speed**.

Beatrix had seen us. She stopped consoling

Grandma. '**What are you doing?**' she screeched.

'We're going to rescue Rose,' I shouted.

'Don't you **dare** fall off,' Beatrix ordered.

'We'll follow on the jet-ski.' Grandma made a dash for the shore.

The camel was just as bumpy as before, though at least this time I didn't have sand in my pants. We **hurtled** along the river path, looking for a cloud of dust in front.

'Where do you think she'll go?' Piper asked.

'I don't know,' I said. 'But I can see where Rose is.' I held up Grandma's phone. 'He swallowed the tracker, remember?'

'I'll take the reins.' Thomas stepped over me. His balance was excellent. 'You shout directions.'

'OK,' I said. 'Keep going straight and speed up.'

The little red dot bounced across the screen. It wasn't heading for the town hall. I watched it closely. 'They're going straight to the tomb,' I said.

'That makes sense,' Piper said. 'She's too squeamish

to mummify him herself. She'll return him as he is.'

'We better hurry then,' I said. **'Can't we go faster?'**

'Would you like to drive?' said Thomas.

'Sorry,' I said.

'I can see the sphinx,' Piper shouted.

'There's Cleo's camel,' Thomas said. 'She's not on it.'

We cantered towards it.

'Where's she gone?' I said.

'**THERE**.' Piper pointed to the biggest pyramid. 'Halfway up. She's heading for the tunnel. She's got the bag.'

'I hope Rose bites her.' I jumped down and raced as fast as I could across the sand, but I wasn't quick enough. I'd barely started to climb when I heard a **SLAM** from above. Cleo had reached the passage and shut the door behind her.

Piper jogged up. 'Don't worry, Ollie. I'm sure we can break in.' She looked up. 'If we can't pick the lock, Thomas can do one of his special kicks.'

'No,' I said. I'd remembered something. I turned and ran towards the dip in the sand. The place we'd been earlier. 'This way.'

'Wait.' Thomas was tying up the camel. 'Where are you going?'

I didn't wait. I didn't know how much time we had. I didn't know if my plan was any good, **but I had to try**.

The gate to the sub-chamber was still open, so I dashed through it and into the passage.

I didn't stop to switch on my torch. I didn't think about the **flesh-eating scarabs**. I just ran as fast as I could.

I reached the wall at the end and threw myself into the gap.

'Blimey, Ollie.' Piper had caught up. She crawled through after me. 'Why have you come down here?'

Thomas stuck his head through. 'What are we doing?' he said.

'There's another tunnel.' I stood and looked

209

around. 'I found it earlier. It might lead to the tomb. If you tip one of the jars, a slab slides back.'

'Which is it?' Piper shone her torch around.

I wasn't sure. I went into the corner and pushed at a few of them.

There was a grating sound. '**This one**.'

'**Wow**.' Piper and Thomas dashed over. Piper looked at me accusingly. 'Why didn't you say anything before?'

'Finding the recipe was more important,' I said. 'I was thinking of Myrtle.'

'You did the right thing.' Thomas gave me a consoling pat. 'And once we've rescued Rose, we'll head straight home.'

We stood around the hole and looked down. The ladder below us plunged into nothing.

'*Blimey*.' Piper peered into it. 'I can't even see the bottom.'

I tried not to think about dead things. 'You don't have to come,' I said. 'I'll be fine on my own.' I lowered myself into the hole and felt for the first rung. 'I'll be back in a bit.'

Piper shone her torch in my face. 'Don't be ridiculous, Ollie. As if we'd let you have all the fun.'

'It wouldn't be fair.' Thomas climbed down after me.

'Thanks,' I said. '**It is a bit dark**.'

211

32

At the bottom of the ladder a passage stretched ahead of us.

It was cold, and damp – and I didn't know silence could be heavy, but it was. I thought of the cosy chamber above, with all its cute little jars. If Piper and Thomas hadn't been with me, I might have scrambled back up.

'Let's go,' I said. I set off into the gloom.

'There's steps at the end.' Piper pointed her torch. 'And another passage. Shall we go up or straight on?'

I held up Grandma's phone so they could see it. 'We're the blue dot,' I said. 'Rose is the red one. They're practically touching.'

'They must be above us,' Thomas said.

The steps were stone, and narrow, and went up in a spiral. They seemed to go on for ever. At last we spilled out into another passage.

'**Blimey**,' Piper crumpled on to the floor. 'Give me a minute.'

'We haven't got time for a sit-down,' I said. 'We must be close.' I looked at the phone again. The red dot was still above us. Now, though, it was darting all over the place. **Ha**. Rose must have escaped.

'Where now?' Piper asked.

I looked right and left down the passage. 'We need more stairs.'

Thomas shook his head. He pointed upwards. '**Look!**' he said. 'There's a hatch in the ceiling. I bet that goes straight to the tomb.'

'**Brilliant**,' I said. I pushed aside the thought of King Tutti-Frutti mouldering in his bandages. 'I'll need something to stand on.'

'Get on my shoulders,' Thomas said.

Thomas is smaller than me, and quite dainty. I gave him a doubtful look. 'Really?' I said.

'Don't worry.' He crouched down. 'We do this in

dance class all the time. It'll be fine.'

I used Piper's head to steady myself while I climbed on. I **wobbled** a bit, but it wasn't as bad as standing on the crocodile.

I pushed the hatch up and peered through it. I couldn't see much,

just shadows and a lot of cobwebs. I did hear **yapping** though, followed by an 'OW' from Cleo. Rose must have bitten her. **Ha**. After the ow, there was more **yapping**, and some muttering, followed by the tap-tap of Cleo's stilettos. It sounded like she was having trouble catching him.

I moved the hatch to one side and reached into the hole. Maybe I could pull myself up, grab Rose and drop back down?

Oh. Maybe not.

Something, about thirty centimetres above my head, was made of solid stone.

'I'm under the sarcophagus,' I whispered down. 'Push me up a bit, Thomas. I'll have to try and wiggle in.'

Oh. I'd barely spoken when something raced towards me.

Something small. Something furry.

Rose! Yay!

He was so pleased to see me, he didn't notice the hole. He dropped straight through it. Luckily, Piper was standing underneath and caught him. **'Yay,'** she said.

'Turn the torch off,' I whispered. I started to wiggle the hatch back into place.

'Anubis?' Cleo called under the sarcophagus.

'Anubis, dear. Come out. I haven't time for games.'

I gave a little **yap**.

'If you won't come out' – she stood back up – 'I shall just leave you here. It'll take a couple of days, but it'll do just as well. **The curse will still be broken**.'

I heard her clopping away.

'Toodle pip, Anubis,' she said.

33

We peered out into the sunshine.

'There she goes,' Thomas said. 'She's left the camel behind. She's taken a tuk-tuk.'

We watched Cleo trundling off in the direction of Cairo. She looked very jolly indeed.

'I expect she's off to a shoe shop.' Piper gave a giggle. 'In readiness for the breaking of the curse.'

'We better find Grandma,' I said. 'She'll be really pleased.'

Just as I said that, Rose sprang from my arms and raced across the sand. He was heading for the café.

'There they are.' Piper pointed.

Grandma and Beatrix were sharing a pot of tea and a plate of syrupy-looking buns.

Well, that was nice. We'd put ourselves in mortal danger, and rescued Rose, and there they were, having a chat.

I stomped over. '**Good of you to come and help**,' I said.

'You didn't seem to **need** any help.' Grandma lifted Rose on to her lap.

Beatrix waved her phone. 'I was tracking you the whole time.'

'By the time we got here' – Grandma poured some syrup over a cake – 'Cleo was out of the pyramid, and we could see you were almost here.'

Beatrix sipped her tea. 'We thought we'd sit and wait.'

'And have a snack.' Grandma took another bun. 'These are **delicious**.'

'Aren't they?' Beatrix took a dainty nibble. 'I can hardly believe they're fat and carb free, Florence.'

'That's what the lady said, Beatrix.' Grandma stuffed one in her mouth. 'She assured me they weren't deep-fried and rolled in sugar.'

'I must get the recipe.' Beatrix reached for another.

'What happened to Geoffrey?' Piper asked.

'They arrested him for the counterfeiting of ancient artefacts.' Grandma tutted. 'I told them all about the amulet.'

'As for Cleo' – Beatrix poured syrup on her bun – 'the high commissioner was **furious** that she's still mummifying dogs. He's on his way to the town hall now.'

'Where's Mina?' Piper asked.

'Gone to gather evidence,' Grandma said.

I felt worried. 'Do you think she's safe?'

Grandma swallowed the last bun. 'It wouldn't hurt to go and check,' she said. 'I'd quite like to say goodbye to Cleo, in any case.'

She brandished her selfie stick.

34

Mina was waiting by the Town Hall gates. She had Ela with her. Piper did her usual thing of going crazy and wishing she could have a pet.

'I didn't have a chance to do much before Cleo turned up,' Mina said. 'I hid for a while and then snuck out the back.'

'What's she doing?' Grandma asked.

'Getting rid of anything that might incriminate her. She's already dumped the dog caskets in the Nile,' Mina said. 'I think she's going to deny everything.'

'**We can't have that**.' Grandma looked indignant.

'Don't worry.' Piper handed Ela back to Mina. '**I've got a plan**.'

Grandma looked miffed. 'I have one too,' she said. 'I was just about to announce it.'

'But mine's really good,' Piper said. 'I only need

Thomas and Ollie and Rose. The rest of you can stay here and cover the exit.'

'Cover the exit?' Grandma's eyebrows shot up. 'Well, Piper, if there's a chance she could escape, your plan might need some work. I'm coming to oversee it.'

Beatrix scowled. **'If Florence is allowed to go, so am I.'**

Piper rolled her eyes. 'All right then. You can all come. Just don't make a noise.'

We tiptoed down to the central chamber as quietly as we could. Cleo had left the doors ajar, and a low humming was coming from inside. Piper peered through. 'She's shredding stuff,' she whispered. 'And she's standing with her back to us. Perfect.'

'Perfect for what?' I asked.

'Your bit.'

'My bit?'

Piper pointed to the roll of bandage suspended over the table. 'You have to attach the end of that to

Rose's collar. Then put him down and come back out.'

'**Eh?**' I stared at her. I didn't get it.

'You'll see.' She turned to Thomas. 'Be ready with the high kicks. Just in case.'

'OK.' Thomas got into position.

'**Go**.' Piper gave me a push.

I did as she said. I tucked Rose under my arm and crawled into the room, up behind Cleo and around the other side of the table.

'What's going on?' Beatrix asked.

'Shhh,' Piper hissed.

Cleo stopped what she was doing and looked over her shoulder.

I took my chance. **I stood up and grabbed the end of the bandage**. I gave it a pull and then crouched back down.

Cleo listened for a moment, then shrugged and turned back to the table. She pushed another document into the shredder.

I tied the bandage to Rose's collar and looked

across at Piper.

She gave me the thumbs up.

I popped Rose down. He looked a bit puzzled, but he didn't try to follow me. I scuttled back to the doorway. 'Now what?' I whispered.

Piper smiled. She pulled her brother's clockwork gerbil out of her pocket. She wound him up, then placed him quietly on the floor.

'**Off you go, Monty**,' she said.

Monty shot off at top speed. Round and round the table he went, his little wheels spinning as fast as they could. Then he did a detour and started zooming round Cleo.

Rose's eyes popped. He stared for a moment, like he couldn't believe his luck. Then he was off too, faster than a speeding bullet. He was going to get that gerbil if it was the last thing he did.

As he ran, the bandage unspooled.

Cleo saw him and gave a little shriek, but she didn't stand a chance.

'She's being **mummified**.' Grandma was thrilled.

'When do I do the high kicking?' Thomas gave an eager *jeté*.

'Sorry.' Piper looked apologetic. 'I don't think you need to now.'

By the time Rose caught Monty, the only bit of Cleo that wasn't bandaged was her head.

She said some very rude things.

Beatrix had to cover my ears.

35

The high commissioner unwound Cleo and took her off to prison. He gave her shoe collection to charity and her job to Mina.

Beatrix kindly paid for the balloon repairs. She said she didn't want me flying home in a **death trap**. I was pleased about that, partly because I hadn't enjoyed plummeting out of the sky, but mainly because we needed to get home as quickly as possible to make the potion. Myrtle was rallying, Mrs Frost said, but she still wasn't a hundred per cent.

We went to see her the second the balloon touched down.

Mrs Frost opened the door with a huge smile. **'Great news,'** she said. **'Myrtle's fully recovered.'**

'Really?' I ran past her into the kitchen. **OMG!** She was right. There was Myrtle on her wheel, her little legs going nineteen to the dozen.

'She looks amazing,' I said. '**Like new**.'

'Doesn't she?' Grandma said, admiringly. 'Practically a different hamster.'

'Was she always that gingery?' Piper asked.

'Yes,' I said. 'She was. Thank you, Mrs Frost.' I gave her a hug.

Walking to Beatrix's, I felt a bit bad for Grandma. We went to all that effort to get the recipe and now Myrtle was fine, and we didn't need it.

Beatrix was home before us. She said she'd parked Dad's plane exactly where he'd left it. 'There's a bit of a scrape down the side,' she said. 'But I'm sure he won't notice.'

●●●

Mum had really enjoyed her surprise anniversary holiday.

'It didn't start well,' she said. 'The airline lost all Dad's luggage.'

'And then' – Dad looked cross – 'the plane was

diverted due to an unexpected monsoon. We ended up in a completely different resort.'

'It had a glorious beach, though,' Mum said. 'I don't think I moved from the sun lounger all week.'

She looked surprised when Beatrix told her Grandma was coming for tea.

'**Florence?**' Mum's eyebrows shot up. '**Really?**'

'She offered to help with the garden.' Beatrix said. 'Said she'd take out my nettles. So kind.'

'That's wonderful.' Mum blinked. 'And how are you, Thomas?'

'Great, thank you, Sukey.' Thomas was wearing Cleo's headdress. 'I'm rehearsing for the show tomorrow. Would you like to see?'

'Very much.' Mum took a seat.

'It's called "Egypt".' Thomas gave a little twirl. 'It tells the story of a great adventure,' he said. 'It's **very** emotional.'

'I'll put the music on, shall I?' I said.

Lots of Thomas's dances start with him in a ball on

the floor, but this one didn't.

This one began with Thomas **running** around the room, **peering** into corners, as if he was searching for something. Then he stood on tiptoe with his eyes shut, making **stabbing** motions. That was followed by some stealthy crawling across the floor.

'I thought he did ballet?' Mum whispered.

'Sadly not,' I whispered back.

It wasn't over. After several vigorous squats, Thomas spun himself into a **glittery** blur. Then he **crumpled** to his knees and mimed weeping, before throwing himself face down on to the rug and remaining motionless.

'Is he OK?' Mum looked worried.

'He's fine,' I said.

Thomas sprang to his feet and pulled off his headdress. 'It's about a high priestess's quest for her heart's desire, and how it eventually became her ruin.'

'**Gracious**,' said Mum.

'She repents at the end, though,' Thomas said. 'Which is good. Did you like it?'

It was definitely one of those occasions where it was OK to lie. 'It was brilliant, Thomas,' I said.

'Yes.' Mum still looked stunned. 'It was. Where do you get your ideas from?'

For a minute I thought Thomas was going to tell her, but he didn't.

•••

Piper came around that afternoon.

She'd brought me something. A certificate.

'I made it myself,' she said.

I could tell.

I read it out.

This certificate certifies that OLLIE BROWN definitely has explorer genes after crash landing in the ocean, riding a camel, walking over crocodiles and crawling through a DARK, scarab-infested tunnel to rescue his Gran's dog!

It looked quite good written down like that. 'Thanks,' I said. 'Though I better not let Mum see it.'

'Probably best,' Piper said.

'I **still** don't like the dark,' I said. 'And I **did** fall off the crocodile.'

Piper shrugged. 'I don't think that matters.'

'How are things at yours?' I asked.

'Good,' she said. 'The twins' teeth have come through. Mum's in a much better mood. *She says I can have a pet.*'

'That's brilliant,' I said. 'What did she say you could have?'

'Whatever I want.' Piper gave a little hop.

'Anything at all?' I blinked.

'As long as it doesn't eat the twins.'

'A gerbil?' I suggested.

'I haven't decided. I'm still thinking about it.'

'The pet shop had some **rats** the other day,' I said. 'Do you want to go and have a look?

•••

Grandma was in the pet shop. She was having an argument with the man at the checkout. 'I don't see why you can't get me a porcupine,' she was saying.

Rose bounced around our feet, **yapping**.

Grandma saw us. 'You're not on your way to the museum, are you?' she said. 'Because I heard they had a robbery.'

'Really?' Piper said.

'**Nothing to do with me, of course**.' Grandma picked a piece of fluff off her collar. 'As I said to the investigating officer, what would I want with old animal teeth?'

I looked at her suspiciously. 'I can't imagine,' I said.

'I guess you've come for hamster food?' Grandma asked. 'I hope you're not after a porcupine?' She gave the man behind the counter a scowl.

'I'm deciding on a pet,' Piper said. 'Mum says I can have one.'

'Really?' Grandma clapped her hands in excitement. '**How about a scorpion?**'

Piper looked thoughtful. 'I'd prefer something with fur,' she said.

'**Fur?**' Grandma blinked. 'In that case ...' She rummaged in her bag. 'This came this morning. Mina sent it. She thought you might be interested.' She held out a photo.

Piper took it.

'Oh,' she said.

He eyes filled with tears.

I looked at the picture. It was Ela.

With six tiny puppies.

'She wanted to know if you'd like one,' Grandma said.

Piper couldn't speak.

'I think she would,' I said.

THE END

Find out how it all began in

GRANDMA DANGEROUS

AND THE DOG OF DESTINY

Out Now!

'What do you mean, you're not taking me?'

I could hardly believe what I was hearing. Was she serious?

'I'm sorry, Ollie.' Mum picked up her suitcase and plonked it on the sofa. 'It's not long till your exams. You can't have time off school before those. They're important.'

'Not as important as going to Clacton,' I said. 'There's a pier there, and an arcade. You have to take me. I love the seaside.'

I may as well not have spoken. Mum turned her back and walked into the kitchen. How rude! I could hear her pulling drawers open. 'Have you seen my sunglasses?' she called. 'I'm sure they were in here.'

I followed her. 'Two weeks won't matter,' I said.

'Two weeks in the whole scheme of things is nothing.' I looked at her, hopefully. 'It'd stop me worrying about Dad.'

Mum stopped rummaging. 'I'm sure Dad would prefer you to stay here studying,' she said.

'No, he wouldn't,' I said. 'Dad doesn't mind about stuff like that.'

'It's not like it's a holiday.'

'It sounds like one.'

'Well, it's not.' Mum popped some mosquito repellent in her bag. 'Poor Aunt Lucy – pecked in the eye by that parrot. SOMEONE has to go and look after her.'

'I didn't even know you had an Aunt Lucy. You've never mentioned her.'

Mum looked a bit flustered. 'Haven't I? She, um, came to stay at Christmas – years ago. Big hair and a fluffy cardi.'

I cast my mind back. Nope. It didn't ring a bell. Still, Mum had loads of aunts. I couldn't be expected to remember all of them.

'I told her safari parks were dangerous,' Mum said. 'Especially in nesting season. Let's hope she takes more notice of what I say in future.'

'You should have mentioned your award.' I said. 'You normally do.'

Mum looked proudly at the enormous trophy on the dresser. 'Don't be cheeky, Ollie. Being voted **Health and Safety Officer of the Year** was a huge honour. You have to admit – Great Potton is a much safer place these days.'

'Much more **boring**, you mean.'

Mum shook her head. 'Skateboards are lethal. So are rollerblades, conkers and chewing gum.

A complete ban was the only way.' She waved vaguely in my direction. 'Pass the sun cream, will you? That's right – the factor 150. You can't be too careful, even in March.'

I handed it to her. 'Please let me come,' I said. 'You can't leave me by myself, I'm only eleven. **It's against the law.'**

'I'm not leaving you by yourself,' Mum said. 'Of course I'm not.' She zipped up her bag. 'Grandma's coming to look after you. She's arriving in the morning.'

Grandma? I stared at Mum in horror. Oh no. Not Grandma Beatrix. I call her Grandma Boring. She's awful. She always goes on about manners, and checks me for nits.

'Unfortunately,' Mum went on, 'Grandma Beatrix is busy, so I had to ask Grandma Florence.'

My mouth fell open. **'Grandma Dangerous?'**

Read the book to see what happens next!

COLLECT THEM ALL!

Nothing is dull while Grandma Dangerous is around!

Kita Mitchell wrote and illustrated her first work, *Cindersmella*, at the age of six. It was cruelly and swiftly rejected by publishers. The sequels, *Repunsmell* and *Mouldilocks*, were equally badly received.

Disheartened, she turned her attention to making stuff, and, luckily, they did degrees in that. After getting one, she built sets for TV shows – but the feeling she should write funny books for children never went away.

Eventually, she decided to have another go. This time, things turned out a little better. Now she can tell people she is a proper author, which is great.

Kita currently lives in Oxfordshire with four daughters and a hamster.

@kitamitchell
www.kitamitchell.com

Nathan Reed has been a professional illustrator since graduating from Falmouth College of Arts in 2000. Recent books include *How to Write Your Best Story Ever* and the *Marsh Road Mystery* series. His latest picture book, written by Angela McAllister, is *Samson the Mighty Flea*. He was also shortlisted for the Serco Prize for Illustration in 2014.

Acknowledgements

With huge thanks to:

Kate Shaw, the loveliest of agents.

Anna Solemani, who I've adored working with.

Nathan Reed, for his most wonderful and hilarious illustrations.

Arvind Shah, who made the series so beautiful.

Dominic Kingston, for enthusiastically organising school visits.

Everyone at **Orchard**, for all being brilliant.

Lorraine, **Rob**, **Jude**, **Neil** and **Ali** for putting up with my complaining.

Claire, **Pete** and **Meryl**, for kindly sharing their in-depth knowledge of Cairo, and bringing me cake.

And of course

Isobel, **Eva**, **Hattie** and **Daisy**, who make everything worthwhile.